Deadline

STEPHANIE AHN

HARRIETTA LEE: DEADLINE

Copyright © 2018 Stephanie Ahn

(Edited: September 2020)

Cover Art and Design © Stephanie and Sarah "Ink" Ahn

All rights reserved. No part of this book may be reproduced or used in any manner without the express written permission of the publisher except for the use of brief quotations in a book review.

This is a work of fiction. Names, characters, businesses, places, events, and incidents are the product of the author's imagination or used in a fictitious manner. Any resemblance to actual persons, living or dead, or actual events is purely coincidental.

ISBN: 978-1-9829-3187-2

www.stephanie-ahn-books.com

DEDICATION

Dedicated to Ink and to my little sister, who saves my life every damn day.

CONTENTS

Content Warnings/Acknowledgments

1	Making Friends	1
2	Pathfinding	17
3	(More Than) Six Feet Under	26
4	Pop! Goes the Weasel	46
5	A Dame with a Mean Backhand	53
6	A Dame with a Meaner Backhand	79
7	Dear Sister	105
8	Is It Hot in Here, or Is That Just the Hellfire?	117
9	The Worst Laid Plans of Demons and Lesbians	137
10	Wrapping Things Up	157
	About the Author	177

AUTHOR'S NOTE
(CONTENT WARNINGS)

This book contains mild violence, adult situations (in the form of consensual BDSM), and the death of a loved one. If this content makes you too uncomfortable, please feel free to stop reading, and I hope you find a book better suited to your wants and needs!

If this is exactly the kind of story you're looking for—carry on!

ACKNOWLEDGMENTS

Special thanks to my earliest readers and editors, Lexi Hoff, Dareen, William Ward, Kshaar, Alexis Brennan, Emily Moraitis, and Anonymous.

CHAPTER 1
MAKING FRIENDS

There's a demon across the street, and she's not being very subtle.

She's wearing nothing but a clean white shift and a grin too wide for a human mouth. Some civilians see her as they pass, but they hastily avert their eyes and quicken their footsteps. I hold her gaze from where I'm standing on the sidewalk, taking in the coils of black hair framing her brown face, the light glinting off her pointed teeth, the way her clothes stretch taut to accommodate wide hips.

I don't have the same brand of people-repellent that she does; a testy businessman clips me with his briefcase as he storms past, throwing me off balance. When I regain my footing and look up from the pavement, she's gone.

She may be expecting me to pursue her, so I don't. Turning my attention back to the tacky, heart-shaped locket in my palm, I watch the traffic for an opportunity, then toss the locket into the street. It disappears under the tires of an oncoming car. There's too much ambient noise for me to hear it crack, but I feel the spell inside it crumble.

One more paycheck in the bag. I'm just barely set to eat and pay this month's rent. But, given how many hours I've worked this week, I think I'm entitled to a day off. I walk away with my hands in my coat pockets, the last whimper of a dying curse still echoing through my head.

***

My cell phone rings while I'm crawling around the floor of my apartment, trying to put out a small fire. I reach for the phone with one hand while flailing to catch my conjured flame with the other; the thumb-sized sprite spits a flurry of sparks at me and hop-skips away, leaving a merry trail of scorch marks across the hardwood. I give up on it for just a second while I fumble with the phone and put it to my ear.

"Hello?"

"Hi Harry!"

"Luce!" I sit up on my haunches, grinning uncontrollably. "What's up?"

"Something cool, actually. Someone wants to hire you."

Well, that's new. It has been a very, very long time since anyone from Luce's circle has stooped to my level. "Are they throwing me another bone?"

"You'd think so, but no. This job actually seems pretty juicy. A messenger of a messenger told me your new client wants to meet in person, give you the details face-to-face."

Huh, that's piqued my interest. I open my mouth to say so when I smell something burning. Shit, my sprite! I swivel back and forth with the phone against my ear, smelling increasingly distressing amounts of smoke. Meanwhile, Luce is still talking.

"How quickly can you get to Café Amara?"

"I—uh—just a second—" The sound of splintering wood grates on my ears. I whip around and curse, seeing the little jackass munch away at one of my desk legs.

"Harry? Harry, what's going on?"

I grab a discarded shirt off the floor.

"Harry, what are you doing?"

"It's fine, I got it!" I shout, my voice going up an octave when the flame lashes out, searing the back of my hand. "Ow! *Shibalsekki!*"

"Oh my gods, are you messing with elementalism again? Harry—"

I drop the phone and hastily wrap my shirt around the desk leg, crushing the sprite within the fabric. It fights me, trying to burn through the shirt to get at my skin again, but even magic fire can't survive without oxygen. I know it's dead when the heat against my palms dwindles.

"Harry? Harrietta!"

Luce's voice is clamoring faintly from the floor. I pick up my phone, more than a little guiltily, and clear my throat. "I got it, nothing to worry about. So, Café Amara?"

I can practically hear Luce shaking her head. "You're going to set yourself on fire one day, and when that happens, I won't be around to save your ass."

It's an automatic reflex, twisting my mouth into a shit-eating grin. "You were there last time, weren't you?"

I wait for the laughing retort, but it doesn't come. Did the connection die? Then the weight of what I've just said hammers me in the ribs, melting the grin off my face. The silence buzzes in my ears like an insect.

When Luce finally speaks, her voice is soft as velvet. "Harry…"

I cringe. Gods, I know she means well, but her tone still makes me nauseous. "Sorry. I shouldn't have mentioned it."

"No, wait—Harry, I'm not upset. This is actually kind of good, you know? Being able to joke about it?"

It is?

"…Yeah. I guess it is."

Another pause. It's not an awkward silence like the last, more of a thoughtful one. The scar on the side of my neck tingles. I give it an idle scratch.

"I'm, uh, heading over to meet the client right now," I mumble. "Talk to you later, okay?"

"Okay. Be safe, sister."

I swallow a lump in my throat. I have to take in a slow breath to speak again. "You too, Luce."

When I hang up, I notice that the shirt I used to smother the sprite now has a hole burnt through it. Son of a bitch.

***

Café Amara is right next to a Starbucks, which sounds like horrible business practice—but that's only if you don't know its role as neutral ground for mages, monsters, and demons alike. First off, it's right in the heart of civilian New York, so causing a disturbance would be bad exposure for everyone. Second, it's owned by the estranged first son of the most powerful werewolf clan in the Northern Hemisphere. And no one wants to piss *those* guys off.

There aren't many people when I get there. I recognize a few members of the community by steaming mugs of beverages that smell oddly like copper, hand-carved talismans jingling on wrists and ankles, and overstuffed beanies concealing more than hair. Also present is a smattering of civilians, gagging and wrinkling their noses at the bad coffee reserved for outsiders. I hold the door open for a couple that barges rudely past me, muttering under their breaths about how they "should've just gone to Starbucks." Gael sees me from behind the counter.

"Hey, Harry," he mumbles in the voice of an

unhappily sober college senior. The creases in his tan forehead are at odds with the cheery green apron tied around his waist. "There's someone waiting for you upstairs." The words are accompanied by a slow, tired blink.

"Thanks. Cup of milk tea, please."

Gael nods curtly and turns around. The russet hair at the back of his head is an uneven mountain range, and he pauses while making the tea to rub a patch of missed stubble on his chin. He brings the tea over, I pay for it, and I take it upstairs without once commenting on his disheveled state.

Upstairs, warm yellow fairy lights compete with the clear sunlight spilling in from outside, winning over all but the chairs and tables right up against the windows. The weathered brown wall paneling is hand-painted with seemingly random, wandering patterns. Tables are spaced out in the center of the room, with more discreet booths along the sides.

A pale, skinny young man, smartly dressed in a blue scarf and gray blazer, sits perfectly still in the corner booth furthest from the stairs. He's staring straight ahead at the empty seat across from him, his hand loosely curled around a full, steaming cup of black coffee. He's trying way too hard to seem relaxed and is probably giving himself a hernia in the process. I hope he's not who I'm supposed to meet.

He sees me and snaps to attention like a spring trap. Oh gods. This is exactly who I'm supposed to meet. My ass isn't even halfway into the booth before he starts talking.

"Harrietta Lee?"

Even as he says my name, his eyes dart towards the collar of my white shirt. The bit of mangled flesh peeking out obviously answers his question, but he waits for my response anyway.

"Yup. Luce said you have a job for me?"

His confusion shows for a brief second, but he blinks it away. "Luce. Lucille. Your sister, yes. We did ask her to put us in contact with you." He turns to pull something from the seat next to him: a simple, brown, letter-sized envelope. "First and foremost, I would ask that you treat this matter with the utmost discretion, as the family involved—"

"Just tell me your name."

The gears beneath his coiffed hair grind to a stop. He manages a halting, "Pardon?"

"Look, I appreciate the effort, but there's no way this is official enough for the fine print to matter. For Christ's sake, you're hiring *me*, and I know that's not a half-assed decision because you people have too much bureaucracy to be making half-assed decisions. So, gloves on, let's get right to putting fingers in holes. Who are you?"

His lower eyelid twitches as he hesitates. I take a sip of my tea.

"...My name is Tristan. I'm an apprentice. Of the Meresti family."

I immediately snort tea up my nose and fall into a violent coughing fit, made all the more embarrassing by the clatter of my cup dropping into its saucer.

"*Seal?*" I demand as soon as I can breathe.

He folds down the sleeve of his blazer and presents a pale, veiny wrist. He screws up his face, concentrating; a design etches itself onto his skin in rich blue ink. It's the silhouette of a bare linden tree with a figure sitting on the lower branches, long hair and skirt waving in the wind. As I keep looking, the branches seem to tremble and alert the figure to my presence. The wind in the scene dies down, letting the figure's hair and skirt drop back toward the ground, and it starts to turn, eyes searching for the observer, for the new supplicant—

I tear my eyes away. Fuck. Of course it has to be the Merestis.

"Nice people," I say, a caustic edge in my voice. "I never got to show my appreciation for the flowers Miriam sent me in the hospital. Thank her for me, will you?"

Tristan's brows knot. He obviously has no clue what I'm talking about. "I'll, er, be sure to relay the message."

I sigh and squeeze my eyes shut. Open them again. "Alright, talk to me. What kind of dirty laundry does your family want me to take out that they can't fix themselves?"

"You're to retrieve something."

He slides the envelope over to me. There's a tingling, gel-like film of invisible wards coating the paper, but it peels back at my touch. Looks like the envelope has been specifically enchanted for me to open. I'm still mad, but I can't say I'm not flattered. The seal breaks like a normal envelope's (I wonder who licked it), and I reach inside to pull out a printed photograph.

The image is that of an ornamental sword, all intricately spun threads of gold and silver twined into a vaguely threatening point. The threads resemble twisting branches, as though someone grew a shrub in a narrow wire cage and metamorphosed it into precious metal. The whole assemblage looks expensive and not at all practical. There are two possible reasons the Merestis would want this back: either the recession hit them hard and they need gold, or the sword has magical properties.

"The sword has magical properties," Tristan explains. "It's been a prime source of the Merestis' prosperity for about eight decades. The story is that Matthew Meresti, our current eldest, ran some favors for a Lithuanian fortune deity back in the day. He eventually named her as his patron and worked her image into our seal. In return, Dalia—the deity—gave him a sword that would guide him and his own to be both avatars and beneficiaries of her will. But the caveat was that the sword and its boon were bound to Matthew's lifetime, so upon his death the family would be made to return both."

"Now he's dying, and you don't have the sword."

Tristan sucks in a quick, sharp breath through his teeth. "Yes."

"And the consequences of that are…?"

"Dalia doesn't just determine the prosperity of human lives, she decides their lengths. If we don't show proper gratitude for the wealth she's provided us, she's entitled to our lifetimes. She might take ten years, or a hundred; it would be different for every individual. The only certainty is that everyone who wears the seal would be affected. And there would be deaths."

My jaw tightens. I think of a delicate brown wrist in my hands, a quiet, murmured explanation in my ear. The way my heart pounded the first time that figure in the linden tree turned to face me, the first time I truly understood what even the likeness of a goddess could do to the human mind—and how what was terrifyingly alien to me was so familiar to Miriam, how she met those immortal eyes with only a warm, respectful fondness and a gentle smile.

All that devotion for a being that would snuff her out over a glorified pigsticker.

"How long has the sword been gone?" I ask.

"A little more than eight hours."

My eyebrows shoot for the ceiling. "Eight hours? You came to me after eight hours?"

Tristan blinks. "Why is that surprising?"

"Well, because I figured I'd be a last resort. Or not a resort at all. Your family's roster is full of the best and brightest, and I *know* you have plenty of fixers on payroll just for emergencies like this. To be honest, I'm—kind of your worst option."

There's a bead of sweat forming at Tristan's

otherwise immaculate hairline. "But you find things, don't you? Search-and-destroy, it's your specialty. Right?"

If possible, my eyebrows shoot higher. "Who told you *that*? Tristan, I'm not a mercenary. My last 'search-and-destroy' was a shitty love spell made by some creepy accountant—"

"—who was stalking the receptionist. I know, I know."

He instantly regrets blurting that out, I can tell. I freeze in place.

"Tristan. Have you been following me?"

I'm glaring razor blades at him, but my mind is taking me back to this morning, to rounded hips and bouncing black hair and a brilliant, fanged grin.

Tristan is floundering. His nervous desperation, barely concealed before, now oozes freely through the cracks. "No! I mean, yes, my family looked you up, that's how I knew—I mean, we knew—I mean—I mean—"

He shuts up, drops his shoulders, and hangs his head. I take a big gulp of my tea. Damn, it's lukewarm.

"Tristan," I say, gently putting down the cup. "Does anybody else in your family know the sword is missing?"

He shakes his head, gelled strands of hair wobbling comically over his forehead. I take a deep breath.

"Did you lose it?"

When Tristan finally looks up, his nose is a lively

shade of pink and his eyes are watering over. Uh oh.

"I—I didn't mean to! They told me it was important, that I just had to get this one package from the vault downtown, I only left it for a second and then it was gone, and I *swear* I looked for it all night and oh god Miriam is going to *kill* me—"

I reach for him, then reconsider as he sniffs up what sounds like a shot glass's worth of snot. Keeping my hands squarely in my side of the booth, I resort to words. "Tristan, don't—look, just calm down—" How do you comfort a preppy white manchild? "Just…breathe. Think about lacrosse. Or something."

Tristan keeps bawling. Even with the discretion charms placed under every table in the café, his blubbering attracts more than a few stares. I try to wait it out, finishing my freezing tea in the process. See, this is why I wish I were better at elementalism; pyros never worry about their tea going cold.

When Tristan's sobbing diminishes into slightly damp sniffling, I figure it's safe to address him again.

"Look, Tristan, you need to tell your family. I wish I could bail you out of this as much as you do, but this is so far out of my league you have no idea. Yes, they'll probably kick the shit out of you, and yes, it'll take years to earn back even a fraction of their trust. But you made a mistake. You *have* to own up to it."

Even as I say the words, the hypocrisy of them stings. If anyone had talked to me like this when I was Tristan's age, I would have shut down like a collapsible tent. It looks like that's exactly what Tristan is doing now; his eyes are glazed over and his mind is obviously far, far away.

"Tristan? Hey, you there?"

Yup, he's not listening. I let out a deep sigh and stand up.

"Go home, Tristan. Tell your family what happened and let them deal with it."

I take my empty cup and saucer and start to step out of the booth, but Tristan's skinny arm shoots out to grab mine. My cup clinks against the saucer as I stumble. "Dude, I told you—"

"Two days. Just look for it for two days, that's all I'm asking." Tristan's pupils are blown wide in his pale blue eyes. Every line in his face screams desperation. "Forty-eight hours, no telling Miriam, that's it."

I blow out a heavy breath through my nose.

"Nope. Sorry."

Somehow, Tristan isn't the least bit deterred. "Okay okay, I understand where you're coming from, but please, I have more—just, don't go—" He lets go of my arm to snatch up the brown envelope still on the table. I should leave, I know that, but I'm curious enough to know what Tristan thinks will change my mind. He fumbles with the envelope, pulls open the mouth with both hands, and presents its contents to me.

Holy *shit*.

"Tristan…" I say, slowly, my voice cracking.

"How much money is that?"

"Thirty thousand."

"Thirty thou—" Oh my gods. Holy shit. Holy fucking shit. "Jesus, kid, where the *Hell* did you get that?"

"Don't infantilize me, I'm twenty-one and you're not that much older. I didn't steal it from the Merestis, I swear. I inherited from my parents just before I cut ties."

I have to sit down. I mean, I don't ever want to think that I'm greedy, but *thirty thousand dollars*. I could do *anything* with that. I could eat *anything*. Go *anywhere*. I could have *savings* in a *bank account*. A question pops into my head and jolts me out of my haze.

"Wait, hold on, what if this Matthew guy dies while I'm still on the job?"

Tristan rolls his eyes. "Matthew Meresti has lived for a hundred and twenty-six years. He's a powerful wizard with a family of the greatest healers and scholars hovering over his bed to pump him full of blood energy every time he so much as sneezes. He's not going to die in two days."

My subconscious has already made a decision, but my rational mind is still in denial. "Kid—I mean, Tristan—you do understand, paying me more isn't going to make me smarter or my magic any stronger, right? Cash is nice, I mean, really, really nice, but I don't have even a fraction of the resources your family has. It's debatable whether I have even a fraction of the resources a *regular* blood witch has.

Are you absolutely sure you want to do this?"

Tristan meets my gaze with equal strength and some exasperation. "It's thirty thousand. I'll live. And if the sword stays gone by the time Matthew Meresti dies, all the money in the world won't save me. I'm paying you thirty thousand, up front, to do your job for two days. You can keep the money whether or not you succeed. But if you do find the sword, I have another thirty thousand waiting for you."

I keep my mouth shut, aware that this is an event horizon. I don't trust myself to say the right thing. So instead, I reach forward and take the envelope.

All of Tristan's intensity dissolves. He deflates with relief, reverting back to the scrawny apprentice who's gotten in over his head. He helps me slide the photograph of the sword into the envelope and watches its brown paper edges disappear into my coat. I feel light-headed.

"So," I say, my mouth forming words without my brain's permission. "How do I contact you?"

"My number is in the envelope. I already have yours."

"Of course you do. Go back home, okay?"

"Okay."

He looks like he's aged forty years since I first saw him. Poor guy. I wish this hadn't happened to him, especially not as an apprentice. Especially not as an apprentice who's already cut ties.

Even as I leave Café Amara, I'm at a complete loss as to how I should approach this job. I'm just one blood mage, and a defective one at that. The extra thirty thousand is most likely a pipe dream, and if the Merestis ever find out I took this deal, they'll collectively kick my ass halfway to the sun. I could tell Luce, maybe get her help—but her sense of responsibility is much healthier than mine, and she'll probably end up convincing me to go to Miriam with the truth. I can't tell *anyone* about this.

The hair on the back of my neck stands up. My scar feels like a dead weight against my skin. I stop, looking around for the source of the uneasiness—but there's no one watching me. At least, not that I can see.

I spin around a few more times, like a doll in a music box, just in case. Was it stupid, taking such a high-stakes job while I've got my own issues to deal with? But then I remember the thirty thousand in my coat pocket, and I decide to hurry home instead of sticking around to tempt fate.

CHAPTER 2
PATHFINDING

I feel safer once I'm in my apartment, within the bounds of the wards I've draped around the building like Christmas lights. It's really not bad for a one-bedroom in Manhattan rented on the salary of a knockoff PI. Entering into the living room which I've converted into an office, I pass between the tiny kitchenette and a door to the bathroom, then face the desk where I do most of my heavy thinking. I toss my coat onto it, squint at the afternoon light encroaching through pleasantly tall windows, then turn right into my bedroom.

I plop down onto my queen bed, ignoring the shriek and wobble of old springs. I hold my breath and take another peek inside the envelope. Wow.

Thirty thousand US dollars. Holy shit. I'm being thrown more than just a bone, this is the whole godsdamned chicken. I hold one of the bills up to the light, then remember that I don't actually know how to recognize counterfeit money. Man, I am so out of my league.

The clock on the wall says it's three thirty; that gives me plenty of time to get started.

I study the photograph as I make my way from the bedroom to the office-slash-living-room. I'd normally begin a job like this with an elementary finding spell, but if it were that easy, I'm sure Tristan wouldn't have come to me. Still, it wouldn't hurt to cover all my bases. And I like setting things on fire.

I get an old-fashioned compass out of my desk drawer, pry the glass lid open with a penknife, and retrieve the needle. I make a copy of the photo in the envelope, and the paper is still warm as I cut out the sword's outline with a pair of kitchen scissors. It would be great if I could use a focus other than a two-dimensional image, but as long as the photo I have is unedited and the sword's appearance is unique enough, I can scrape by. I drip a divining sigil onto a frying pan with candle wax — then scrub the whole thing off, because the pan is still crusted with spaghetti sauce from yesterday's dinner. Oops. I craft the sigil again, sans marinara this time, then prick my finger with a sanitized sewing needle and squeeze a drop of blood onto it. I lay the cut-out photo over the sigil, then cordially introduce it to the open flame of a lighter.

It's an explosive union. Sparks fly, and errant ashes drift down to coat the kitchenette counter. What remains is a small, steady, snow-white flame. Despite its odd appearance, it functions the same way as any other fire; I hold the compass needle over it and let the flat metal surface bloom black and brown from the heat. When the fire's consumed all of the photograph, I place the needle back inside the compass along with a sprinkle of ash, just for good measure.

Nothing happens. Until I replace the glass lid.

The compass needle comes to life, whirling in a dizzy frenzy that makes me start and jump back. I… wasn't expecting this to work. Hoping, maybe, but not expecting. Maybe Tristan is so much of a nervous wreck that he didn't think to try the simplest solution before running to me with his parents' money… No, that's not right. Tristan may be desperate, but he's not stupid. The Merestis don't stamp that seal onto just anyone's wrist.

So maybe it's not Tristan—maybe it's me. My magic hasn't been quite right ever since the incident, and I'm still adjusting to the ways it's changed. Maybe, just maybe, the sword is stuck inside a complex Faraday cage of concealing wards, but my fucked-up magic is letting me slip through the gaps.

But none of that really matters. What matters is that I made a promise, and I have a lead. Also, thirty thousand dollars.

Thirty fucking thousand. Wow.

I take the compass off the kitchenette counter and

back to my bed, fishing a candy bar out of my coat along the way. Ah, chocolate, always good for broody contemplation. I could call Miriam and tell her what's going on... my noisy munching slows, and I chase the idea off my property with a broomstick. I don't want to talk to Miriam, and I'm damn sure she doesn't want to talk to me. If she finds out that I know about the Merestis' current weakness, she's more likely to throw me in her family's dungeon—which I've never seen, but am sure exists—than to let me help. After all, she does put her family before her friends, and I'm not even a friend anymore. Maybe I never was.

With that dismal thought, I immediately begin choking on peanut butter and caramel filling.

I toss the wrapper out and start pacing back and forth between my bedroom and office, turning the compass over and over in my hands. The only problem with my crude finding spell is that it shows direction but not distance; the sword could be two miles or two thousand miles away, and I wouldn't be able to tell the difference. Following this lead first means I could waste an entire evening on what's already a time-sensitive job... On the other hand, if the sword is stuck in an iceberg somewhere in Alaska, this whole thing is already a hopeless endeavor.

Might as well get back to work then. I shrug my coat back on, checking the inner pockets to make sure I've got my essentials. Glasses, penknife, razor blades, matches, tampons, etc. I pull my hair back with a new elastic, adjust my blood red tie, and head outside.

***

Compass in hand, I trot merrily down the sunlit streets of Manhattan. The metal and glass walls rising up to my left and right make me feel like I'm at the bottom of an enormous artificial canyon. It's a comforting feeling, similar to what I used to get in Seoul, but with an ever-present dusting of foreignness. The buildings are bigger, the people are shinier, the cars are noisier—just under two years as a resident, yet this city still makes me feel like a tourist.

According to the digital compass in my phone, the magical compass is pointing due east—not that I really trust my phone, ever since it mysteriously posted a nude to my Facebook and got me banned for life. I walk a couple blocks north, then check both compasses again; the magical needle has moved a few ticks south of its original direction. Now, I may have failed high school trigonometry, but at least I know that means the sword *isn't* on a different continent. Hell, with an angle change that noticeable, it might even be within walking distance. That extra thirty thousand might be in reach after all... okay, so let's get walking.

My little compass attracts a few questioning glances, but nothing more. I, on the other hand, am a magnet for unsought attention. For about a minute I walk behind a man with a toddler glued to his chest; the kid's eyes are like satellite dishes the whole time, fixated solely on the scar at my throat. I escape the visual inquisition by taking cover in a bakery, and as payment for safe quarter I leave the tip jar jingling.

A street vendor sells me a bottle of water somewhere around 53rd Street. I bring it to my lips just as a familiar head of dark, springy curls whisks by — the water dodges my mouth and drenches my shirt instead. I curse, and the head in question turns around to reveal a decidedly human woman I've never seen before. She's very attractive actually, and the raised eyebrow she points at my soaked shirt pains my ego. Ah well, I'll live.

By the time my shirt dries, the sky is darkening rapidly. I wait at a crosswalk for the traffic light to change, checking my compass in the meantime. The needle points straight ahead, up the avenue to the north. I consider taking the subway back home. I've been walking for almost three hours now, and all I have to show it for it is a growling stomach, a ruined tie, and a pair of aching feet. Maybe it's time for a different tactic.

As I deliberate, the light changes to green and the crowd around me begins to shuffle forward. Oh well, I've already come this far. A few more blocks won't kill me. I take advantage of my long legs, speeding ahead of the others on the street. About halfway across, I take a passing glance at the compass.

I stop. The scorched needle is spinning dizzily,

unable to decide on one direction. I rap on the glass with my knuckles, shake it around. The needle remains indecisive. As people shoulder past me, I puzzle over the new development. Is something interfering with the signal? Maybe whoever has the sword found out I was tracking them? The glare of the setting sun against the glass is Hell-bent on blinding me; I tilt the compass to avoid it.

Wait. I tilt the device again, this time holding it vertically like a clock face. The red-tipped end of the compass plunges downward, leaving the needle in a perfectly vertical, gravity-defying position. Holy *shit*.

An obnoxious *BEEEEP* to my left shakes me out of my haze. A surrounding chorus of car horns chimes in, as well as a few angry, mostly male shouts muffled by closed car windows. I check the area around my feet one more time, praying for any additional clues, but I come up empty. A driver in a black sedan sticks his hand out the window to flip me off. I return the gesture, then scamper across the street before he can run me over.

I spend the next two hours investigating the area, trying to find out what's below the street—basements, parking garages, subway tunnels, anything—but no matter how much I snoop and poke around, nothing ever leads me to the exact spot indicated by the compass below street level. In fact, subway maps and building blueprints indicate something of a void there, conveniently untouched by habitable human construction. I search for trick walls, concealed stairways, hidden hatches—but I always wind up right back in the middle of the crosswalk, confused and unable to do anything but stare at the little device in my hand.

There's one more possibility I'm actively ignoring, mostly because it's way too cartoonish. There's an open manhole in the sidewalk right by the compass hotspot, marked out with bright orange tape and cones. Three maintenance workers in garishly yellow vests are popping in and out like bumblebees visiting a hive. I've walked past them so often in my futile search that they're giving me annoyed looks.

Sewers. It's probably not the only option left, but it is the most undesirable, which automatically ranks it higher as a possibility. That's the great thing about having generally shitty (pun intended) luck— you start being able to predict the future based on how little you want to face a specific outcome. And my sinking dread at the prospect of trudging through a dank sewer probably means it's inevitable.

Or... I could call Miriam.

Nope. Not happening. I stand on the sidewalk as afternoon bleeds into evening, watching the maintenance workers close up the manhole and gather up their orange cones. One gives me a dirty look; it occurs to me that my loitering might come off as rude, even creepy. Woops. I hastily turn the street corner.

Whatever I need to get into those sewers, I'm

going to get.
 Miriam doesn't need to know a thing.

CHAPTER 3
(MORE THAN) SIX FEET UNDER

The moon is out when I return to the spot. I find a manhole in a dirty alley nearby, out of the curious public's view. Once I'm sure I'm alone, I pull my crowbar out from where it's creating an all-too-conspicuous tent in my backpack.

The sharp, hooked end barely fits into the holes in the manhole cover, and it takes a lot of wiggling and stomping to get it properly inserted (laugh it up, Sigmund Freud). Once the hook is in, I wiggle some more, then brace myself and pry the cover open.

Fuck, it's heavy. I have no chance of lifting it, not with my muscles, so I shove it to the side with the sound of scraping stone. The crowbar goes back into my backpack; it's been a staple of my more physically demanding adventures for a little less than a year now, ever since a football player tried to brain me with it. Ah, memories. I hook a black surgical mask over my ears, one with a purifying sigil stitched onto it with white thread. Who *knows* what kind of toxic fumes New York City sewage emits.

I check the rest of my backpack's contents as well. I'm wearing a heavy-duty raincoat without my usual plethora of pockets, so everything I usually keep in my coat is in the bag. I brought a few extra knickknacks as well—for instance, an emergency concussion hex in a jam jar, crafted with the explosive rage harnessed from last week's Red Sox vs. Yankees game and lovingly cocooned in bubble wrap. I'm not a softball lesbian, but I don't mind impersonating one to get straight friends to pay for sports tickets.

I scuff my boots against the ground, strap on a headlamp, and pull on a pair of thick gloves. I take a deep, deep breath, then slip into the manhole.

I move down the ladder slowly, feeling for the next rung with each foot before descending. The crowbar in my backpack keeps shifting, hitting the tunnel wall with a muffled *clang* and dragging noisily as I continue my descent. Then there are no more rungs left, and my boot sinks into cold, thick, swirling liquid. I turn around, bringing light into the darkness.

The tunnel is less cavernous than as advertised by the Ninja Turtles, but it's still big enough to stand upright in. The concrete walls curve out, then up, forming a nice, symmetrical circle. The steady beam of my headlamp gets lost in the seemingly unending length of darkness. I can already tell that wandering around with my compass won't do me much good, so I click off my headlamp and pull out my glasses.

As soon as the lenses settle over my eyes, the darkness is irrelevant. I see the tunnel in energy — flowing with the water at my feet, worming through the tiniest cracks in the walls, thriving in the microbes that cover every surface. I raise my hand in front of me; my own veins glow bright red, the light pulsing in time to my heartbeat. I place my palm against the wall, take it off, and see the faintest, shimmering smudge of scarlet I've left on its surface. The sight makes me nostalgic for the glow-in-the-dark stars I had on my ceiling as a kid.

Looking down the tunnel, I see everything this place is and everything it has been. I see faint imprints detailing the way it's changed, the ways the water has risen and fallen, the walls crumbled and patched up. Wavering echoes of scarlet blood energy, like ethereal ghosts, speak of passing maintenance workers and the occasional urban explorer. And something... else?

The flickering trail in front of me speaks of a living organism, fluttering down the tunnel and then taking a sharp turn to disappear into the wall. I follow it to that spot, squelching through the water and feeling the warmth of my breath trapped inside my mask. There's a blazing patch of unstable energy on the concrete wall where it must have seen recent change. It's in the rough shape of a circle, coming up from just above water level to my shoulders, too neat to have been a natural collapse. Not to mention that, with my glasses off and my headlamp on, it becomes completely invisible. Alright, I'll bite.

I scour the area, looking for a hidden switch, rune, or sigil of some kind, some type of trigger to open the passageway, but even with my glasses I detect nothing. Then, by chance, I look down. Just at the level of my knees is a spot of swirling, concentrated energy. I crouch and push against it with my hand; it sinks slightly into the wall, then slides to the left.

The circular doorway collapses in on itself. I stumble back as the concrete crumbles into a pile of loose, small rocks that burst outward—then freeze in place, looking like a single frame in a stop-motion animation. I poke one of the rocks; it remains suspended and unmoving in space.

Now *that's* cool.

Looking down the newly-opened passageway immediately gives me a headache. The whole place is a mess of fluctuating energy, echoes of tunnels and organisms of the past all jumbling together in a mix of colors and signals I can't tell apart. I hastily pull off my glasses, click on my headlamp, and the chaos reorganizes itself into a long, narrow tunnel branching in four different directions just ahead.

I enter, ducking down so that my backpack brushes the ceiling. The doorway seems to sense when I pass through it; there's a sound like a cascade of pebbles down a driveway, then larger volumes of grinding and colliding rock. When I twist around, all I see is a solid wall. I face the tunnel again and move forward.

When I get to the fork, I check my compass and see that the indicated tunnel is only as high as a toddler. That's not going to work. I go through the closest one to the right, which allows me to stand upright with just a bit of a slouch.

I keep going that way, entering tunnels based on whether they extend in the general direction the compass points, as well as whether or not I can actually fit into them. I'm a little worried that all the tunnels leading to the sword may be too small, and I'll just end up circling around and around it until I keel over from vertigo.

I'm creeping through a tunnel that's just about as high as I am, looking down at my compass, when an enormous scratching, rumbling noise starts deep in the wall to my right. I turn toward the wall, illuminating the rough concrete just in time for it to explode with chunks of rock, a few hitting me in the face and chest. From the newly made hole, a face peeks through.

The face and I stare at each other for a good second. I'm… not even sure if it's a face. It has a flat, pink nose fringed with finger-sized tentacles, leading up to a scaly, asbestos-white snout as wide as my own head. There's a distinct lack of eyes.

Then the face whistles, high-pitched and piercing

straight through my eardrums like a needle. I stumble back to the other side of the tunnel, then do the smart thing and run.

The tunnel lights up with more whistles, clicks, and other unearthly noises. The hairs on the back of my neck stick up like spines, my skin crawling with every skitter and rumble that reaches me through the walls.

The ground behind me thunders, and I twist around just in time to see a body of white burst through. The bouncing, unsteady light of my headlamp reveals—an alligator? It has the leathery hide and long snout, but its feet are huge and flat like oven mitts. It shuffles toward me at an alarming pace, opening its jaws to reveal rows upon rows of jagged teeth. It lunges—I turn fully toward it, drop to one knee, and raise my forearms over my eyes.

My shield goes up just as the thing reaches me. It bounces off the invisible, curved surface, its momentum throwing it to the side so that it hits the ground belly-up, keening like a wounded dog. My shield falls to tatters not a moment after; I readjust my headlamp, get to my feet, and resume running.

I check my compass at the next fork, but the tunnel that leads in that direction has rock dust billowing out of it like smoke out of a chimney, and I can hear heavy bodies shuffling within. The tunnel next to it is about five feet high and a little wider than my shoulders—I throw myself into it. There's a smaller tunnel branching immediately off to one side, so I drop to my hands and knees and squeeze in, hoping to throw the creatures off. They have to be some kind of chimera; they look too similar to Earth creatures to be from anywhere else.

Rumbling—something like a bear trap closes on my foot. I roll onto my back and see another chimera head popping out of the ground, its jaws clamped tight around my boot. I feel the tips of its teeth breaking through the rubber, sinking into skin and stringy muscle. Blood wells up through my pants, and my entire leg seizes up with numb, half-realized pain—I flounder in my own head until I can get ahold of the sensation, force it down the length of my arm and gather it into my hand. It crystallizes, taking visible form as a translucent blade, like a shard of ruby stained glass.

The chimera yanks me toward it with a toss of its head. I follow the momentum, throw myself forward, and bury the shard in the top of its snout.

It opens its mouth to scream—gods, the noise—and I scramble away using mostly my uninjured foot, adrenaline masking the agony long enough to keep me moving. The small tunnel opens into a bigger passageway stretching left and right, and I gladly let myself tumble into it—but I realize a beat too late that the tunnel slopes sharply downward.

I go into an undignified slide. I try to find a handhold, and the rough rock punishes me by ripping off my glove and mercilessly scraping the hand underneath. My backpack gets caught on something and is torn from my shoulders. Eventually, I just let gravity take me, curling up to protect my face until level ground rushes up to greet me with a rib-shaking *THUMP*.

I unfurl carefully, wincing at all the cuts and scrapes that have opened up across my body. My pulse pounds heavily in my wounded ankle, and I can feel my sock soaking with blood. My hand stings. My lungs are burning. My mask fell off my face somewhere, so all the dusty air I've inhaled has settled thickly in my throat. I wait for my vision to clear, for the murky shadows to recede and reveal the bright beam of my headlamp. But the darkness remain complete.

Fuck. I knock on my headlamp with bloody knuckles and get no response. Fuck fuck fuck. I'm so fucked. *Shibal!* I grope blindly around me, nearly fainting from relief when I feel the familiar fabric of my backpack. I slide my palms over it until I find the front pocket, fumble with the zipper, and find my glasses. I run my fingers across the plastic frame to figure out which way is up, then put them on.

The world lights up in a haze of magical energy. Strong, active magical energy, not the potential kind that exists in everything. Stuff that follows in the wake of practiced magic. I'm not in a tunnel anymore; this is a room. It must be old, because my glasses detect settled, stable energy sunken deep into the long-undisturbed rock. I watch the swirling patterns of magic way above me, at once mesmerized by the prettiness and considering the possibility of a concussion. Then I hear snuffling, shuffling, bits of rock coming loose and tumbling down the tunnel I've just fallen through.

I grab my backpack and shove myself away from the wall. The sloped tunnel I came through is wide but not tall, its mouth only taking up a fraction of the massive wall it occupies. I dig desperately through my pack—there's no way I'm defending myself from a squadron of enormous chimeras with just a crowbar, and it's unlikely they'll accept candy bars as a peace offering. My panic rises as I hear the sounds get closer. Then my hands land on a mass of plastic bubble wrap with a smooth, glass surface peeking out. I tear open the bubble wrap and pull free my jam jar hex; its insides simmer with pent-up, volatile energy the color of yellowcake.

I get to my feet, stumbling on my bad leg, and wind back. The tips of a chimera's claws become visible at the mouth of the tunnel—I imagine that they're a catcher's glove, that the underground rock I'm standing on is actually a pitcher's mound, and that there's an entire stadium holding its breath with me as I tighten my scraped-up fingers around the ball. The claws shift; I throw.

My vision explodes with colors that have no name in the English language. The sound of rupturing rock and tinkling glass are drowned out by chimera screams, hoarse and strangled and rattling my eardrums at a frequency that seems to split my head in two. I fall to the ground, covering my ears and squeezing my eyes shut, all my senses overloaded.

...The whining in my ears fades after what feels

like forever. I hear a few final wails from the chimeras, the skittering of smaller pebbles. When I open my eyes, one of the lenses of my glasses is cracked, placing a blurry line dead center in my vision. When I look up, the mouth of the tunnel has been replaced by a wall of crumbled rock; it glows fluorescent with the remnant energy transferred into it by my hex.

I put my backpack on and get to my feet. The ceiling is higher than I thought it would be, cavernous even. I raise my arms over my head. Gods, it feels good to stretch. Then I finally see where all the magical hubbub is coming from.

There's a pedestal hewn from rough rock in the center of the room, topped with a glass display case. When I get closer, I can see something inside the glass glowing with enough silvery energy to blind. The object itself is tiny, thin, and about as long as my pinky finger. It looks like a needle, or…

A sword. It's the Merestis' godsdamned sword. I get out my compass and, sure enough, the needle points straight forward. No fucking way. Tristan, you dense motherfucker, you couldn't have at least told me the *size* of this thing?

I adjust my glasses, squinting through the blurriness caused by both the lens damage and the blinding energy. The sword is levitating a few inches off the actual pedestal, which I now see is etched with all sorts of protective wards. Magic rises up from the wards to coalesce into a thin, translucent sphere surrounding the sword like an iridescent soap bubble.

I get out my crowbar, planning to pry the glass case open like any other civilized tomb raider. Then I consider the fact that it'll be more satisfying to smash it. So I do.

Once the glass is gone, some of the trapped magic dissipates into the air. There's still the small matter of the ward bubble to take care of. I poke it with the tip of my crowbar; upon contact, it transforms from its liquid, elastic form into an impenetrable solid, and my crowbar skids off its surface. Okay, so it's meant to keep things out, not burn the living shit out of someone who puts their hand through. Good to know.

I check my compass again, shaking it a bit to make sure it's really functioning. The bubble should be blocking any finding spells, including the one in my hand. So either the bubble is malfunctioning, or it's making an exception for me and my corrupted magic.

"Only one way to find out," I mutter to myself.

I pull my remaining glove off and drop it to the floor, then rub my palms together, just for extra luck. I reach for the bubble with the tip of a finger. The second I touch its surface, the bubble bloats like a tumor, its perfectly even shape swelling and distorting in all the wrong places. Was this a mistake? The bubble caves away from my touch, shrinking away like a frightened child.

And then it just… pops.

The little sword clatters to the pedestal's surface.

I pick it up gingerly between my thumb and forefinger, feeling the texture of all its intricate details. I reach into my backpack for my needle case, a miniscule cloth book lined with a thick layer of pincushion material, and nestle the sword in among its cheaper, less mystical kin.

I think I hear chimeras in the walls again. There's a tunnel, other than the one I collapsed, directly ahead; I run in its direction. By the time I reach it, the walls are definitely coming alive.

These tunnels are taller than the ones I crawled through earlier. Maybe they're actually meant for people? I've never seen a chimera intelligent enough to construct a ward set as complicated as the ones in the previous room. On the other hand, I've never seen any chimeras like these before, so anything is possible — including the clawed foot bursting out of the ceiling ahead of me, swinging in a deadly arc toward my face.

I dodge just in time to avoid losing my nose, but a claw rips a line across my cheek before glancing off the hard plastic of my headlamp. Breaktime's over, I'm back in flight mode.

This time, as I run through the tunnels, I feel my heart chill over with a profound sense of dread. The simple fact is, I don't know where I'm going. I don't know how to get out of here. My compass is useless now that its objective is tucked into my backpack. I reason that if I find tunnels that slope upward, toward more unstable energy, I might be able to find my way back into the sewers. Gods, it's cold — I was sweating earlier, but now my clammy skin feels like it's frosting over. And though I haven't run into any chimeras since the one that tried to take off my face, I can hear them getting closer through the walls. Once they find the tunnel I'm in, I won't be able to outrun them.

I need a plan. I reach a fork, but it's not really a fork because the tunnel that leads to the left is a dead end. It sort of dips downward before coming to a stop; I think I can hide in there, just for a bit. I hop into the hole, crouching down and finding that, even with my height, it conceals all but the top of my head.

I extract a matchbox from my bag. The bleeding in my ankle is close to staunched, but the trickles of blood running down my cheek still hold pulses of life. I touch the crusting liquid with my fingertips and smear it onto the tip of a match, where it glows in a pulsating rhythm. I strike twice against the matchbox before I get a spark. The light is blurred and distorted by the crack in my glasses, but it's a welcome sight all the same.

The flame wakes up, little by little, yawning and blinking and thinking to do nothing but consume the rest of the match at its own, leisurely pace. I hold another match against the first, and the newborn sprite eagerly gobbles that up too. Usually, I'd spend more time pampering the sprite, maybe feeding it another match, but right now I don't have the luxury of time. I blow lightly on the flames, making the sprite waver, scaring it into paying attention. I feel a little guilty about panicking it like that, but it did chew a hole through one of my nicest shirts.

There's a food source not far from here, I tell it. My blood is its blood; it understands what I'm saying even if I don't speak out loud. *It's down that tunnel—* I direct it at the passageway I haven't been through yet—*it's dry and tasty and it'll make you strong. Go find it, go!*

The sprite launches itself off the blackening matches with adventurous vigor, and for a second I'm terrified that it'll hit a patch of damp earth and extinguish itself.

But my little flame is smarter than that. It skitters lightly across the dangerous terrain, leaping for the driest surfaces, fixated on nothing but the lie I've fed it. It won't last very long, especially in a cold, dank environment like this, but hopefully it'll distract the chimeras long enough for me to come up with a plan.

The sprite looks a bit like a pixie actually, flickering in the distance like that. Maybe I should give it a name.

But no time for that now. I hunker down to brainstorm a way out of these damn tunnels. Maybe if I wander long enough, I'll find the path I entered through and be able to follow the smudges of energy I left earlier. But I've been running like a headless chicken for a while, and I'm pretty sure I've crossed my own path multiple times. Trying to backtrack will most likely get me even more hopelessly lost. Maybe I should build another finding spell? But even a simple directional spell takes time, and if I try to repurpose the compass I already have, I'll be torn apart by chimeras in my little crafting nook.

A highly improbable, grandly simplistic idea occurs to me. I pull out my compass, then my needle case. I wonder...?

When I open the needle case, the Merestis' sword still glows silver, but not quite so violently as before. Instead of blasting outward, its power now thrums up and down the threads of precious metal that make up its blade. It's restrained, compact, like... a battery, is the best way I can put it. And batteries... fit into things, right?

My conjured shards can't interact with anything non-organic, so I get out my penknife to remove the compass's glass cover again, as well as the scorched magnetic needle. The sword seems just about the right size to replace it, and its fancy design means it has plenty of grooves for fixing it onto the fulcrum. Of course it's not balanced, nor is it as light as a regular compass needle; it lies listlessly against the painted letters inside the compass, inanimate. If a tiny sword could have depression, this one would be on 40 milligram Prozac pills. I suck in a deep breath and replace the glass cover with the smallest *click!*

The sword remains dead. The child in me wants to hurl the compass at the wall, but the survivalist in me steadies my hand. *Breathe*, I tell myself. And when I do, a strange, unexpected scent cuts through the dirt and damp to slip into my lungs. Is that...

honey and lemon peel? It's as strong as perfume, like someone wearing the scent is right behind me, leaning over my shoulder with their hair brushing up against mine. And I feel a familiar feeling, this... overwhelming, fearful respect that's only ever gripped me while I stared at the tattoo of the figure in the linden tree, its blue ink skirt blowing in the wind. Linden trees... they smell like honey and lemon peel, don't they? I feel compelled to turn around—no, something *wants* me to turn around. To turn around and face her, to offer my service, the tick-tick-ticking years of my petty, mortal life—

The sword perks up.

It defies gravity, balancing in a perfectly horizontal line inside the compass. It moves, slowly at first and then gaining momentum, until its tip is lined up with the tunnel opening just ahead.

I forget everything else and scramble to my feet, climbing out of my hidey-hole and hurrying to where the sword points until I'm standing right in the middle of the previous fork. The sword swivels much more quickly than it did before, pointing distinctly toward the tunnel I just came through. Holy shit, I might actually get out of this alive.

Something twinkles at the corner of my vision. I spin, expecting a chimera's alabaster hide, and instead find my little living flame skipping circles around my feet. It crackles happily. Though I could be imagining things, it seems to have gotten much fatter than when I first created it.

Shit. I didn't mean for the flame to sustain itself

long enough to come back to me. Somewhere in these godsforsaken tunnels, it must have actually found something to eat. If the chimeras were chasing it, that means they'll be led straight back to—

The tunnel I sent the sprite through earlier echoes with screeches, whistles, and clicks. I take off sprinting in the other direction.

I spend the next few minutes alternately running, hobbling, and crawling at breakneck speed, pain and fatigue pushed aside in favor of blind faith in the device I hold in my hand. I never have to stop and wait for the sword to pick a direction; every time I check it, it's already telling me where I need to go. My reliance on it grows the further I run. The tunnels are getting fresher and marked by more recent change, causing dizzying overlaps between real tunnels and illusions of past ones. Even the compass itself is getting harder to see with all the frantic running and cracked glasses.

Surprisingly, I run into little to no chimeras. The ones I do cross paths with seem to reach me just a second too late, dropping into tunnels I've just crawled out of or poking their tentacle-nosed snouts through patches of ground fresh with my footprints. It's all the sword's doing, I'm sure. If this is what the Merestis have had up their sleeve for decades, it's no wonder they're one of the most powerful mage families in the country today.

My vision gets messier as I approach the newest tunnels closest to the surface. Eventually, I can't see through the chaos at all. Everything hinges on the compass now. I recklessly throw myself in whichever direction it points, praying every second that I don't smash into unyielding rock.

And then I smell something I never thought I'd be glad to smell: sewage. I would sob with relief if I had the breath to spare. I glance down at the compass and look up just in time to realize I'm about to hit a solid wall—I raise my shield, and plow through.

I crash-land into a river of sewer water, twisting around as I land to keep the compass and most of my face dry. The smell is overpowering. I gag once before I force myself to stop breathing, splashing awkwardly toward the same ladder I used to gain entry before.

My hand slaps against a metal rung just as a huge *SPLASH* echoes behind me. I don't even turn to look, just clamp the compass between my teeth and start hauling myself up the ladder. My waterlogged clothes weigh me down, my vision is still an incoherent mess, and I yelp and almost topple off the ladder when my head hits the manhole cover. I brace one hand against it—am I hearing more splashing behind me?—and push.

It barely budges. Son of a—I unhook my foot from the ladder and *slam* my injured ankle against the metal rung. The dull, throbbing ache roars back up into a screaming storm; I let it flood the veins of my arm as I push the manhole cover again.

It lifts clear. I shove it to one side, then start to pull myself through.

I take a huge gulp of oxygen as soon as my head clears the opening. Oh gods, sweet, sweet, polluted city air. It's like a party in my lungs—then I nearly lose my footing on the ladder as the whole structure vibrates. A glance downward through my glasses reveals flashes of angry, living red plowing through churning violet liquid.

Nope. Nope nope nope. I don't know if chimeras can climb ladders and I'm not willing to find out. I start clambering out of the manhole, dragging my torso out onto the asphalt road.

I hear rumbling. Not rock-rumbling, motor-rumbling. I look to one side and find myself blinded by headlights.

Oh, *fuck* no.

It takes me half a second to decide between up or down—an unearthly whistle wafting up from below, an extra vibration of the ladder, and I choose up. I scrape my knees on the lip of the manhole as I scramble out, screaming, not sure if I'm trying to startle myself into moving faster or alert the car's driver to my presence. I clear the manhole and roll—roll all the way to an empty patch of sidewalk, still confused by the energy vision, unsure of which way is up, fueled entirely by pain and panic and pain.

I flop onto my stomach on the curb. The dry concrete against my cheek is bliss. I feel like shit. I smell like worse shit.

But the compass is still held tightly between my teeth. I spit it out and turn over onto my side to get a good look at it. I'm immediately bombarded by an image of swirling, argent-white power—I tear my glasses off and look again. The glass is filthy with rock dust, but when I wipe the grime off with my wrist, I see the sword is still safely nestled inside.

I let my head *thunk* back onto the ground, arms folding protectively around the compass. I have to call Tristan. Tell him I found it, tell him the job is finished, tell him dear gods please never, ever, *ever* contact me again. My hands shaking, I grope an inner pocket of my backpack for my phone. It's definitely still there, I can feel the weight—oh. When I pull it out, the screen is shattered and bent like a tin can.

The gods can only do so much, I guess.

CHAPTER 4
POP! GOES THE WEASEL

It takes two showers and three decontamination rituals before I feel remotely clean enough to sit on my bed. It'd be too much work to salvage my clothes and backpack, so those have been tossed into a massive garbage bag and disposed of. My ankle is now heavily disinfected and swathed in bandages, and my cheek has been patched up with the biggest Band-Aid I could get ahold of. Well, I wouldn't quite say "patched up." The Band-Aid isn't big enough to cover the entire wound, so at the moment it just seals the two slabs of skin together like a line of staples. Maybe I'd be better off getting stitches… but no, that would require a hospital.

I'm sure I'll be alright. I may have lost my ability

to heal with blood magic, but I've still got a kickass immune system. I think.

I hold the sword in my hands, turning it over in my palm and tracing the intertwining metal with my fingertips. All that trouble over something so small. All I have to do now is pick up the landline phone on my desk and call Tristan to let him know I have it. Thirty thousand dollars, just like that.

But I have questions. Who stole the sword in the first place? I highly doubt it was the chimeras, unless Tristan is so oblivious he somehow missed a giant albino lizard with a tentacle nose crawling out of the gutter next to him. How did my finding spell detect the sword through the ward bubble? What is going *on*?

Tristan's number, as promised, is on a little white card inside the brown envelope. I raise my eyebrow at the unnaturally artistic handwriting. If Tristan ever quits magic, at least he'll have a promising career as a calligrapher. When I dial the number into the phone, my ear is assaulted by Eminem's "3 A.M." After a few more seconds of eardrum torture, Tristan picks up.

"Who is this?" he says.

"Hey Tristan. It's Harry."

"Oh, it's you! I've been trying to reach you for an hour!"

"Yeah, sorry. My cell phone kind of died on me."

"Well I'm glad you called, I have a lead—"

"I found it."

A pause. Then, an uncomprehending, "What?"

"Yeah, the sword. I'm holding it right now."

He's quiet. Then, "You... you actually found it? I—I need to see it in person. Meet me at..."

***

When I walk into the dimly-lit alley where Tristan and I agreed to meet, I find him looking even twitchier than the first time I saw him. He keeps running his hand through his hair, fiddling with the buttons on his blazer, and scuffing the pavement with his expensive Oxfords. I don't mean to sneak up on him, but he jumps at the sound of my footsteps. When he sees that it's my face in the shadows, he sags in relief.

"Where is it?" he demands.

I produce the needle case from my coat pocket and start to open it. He scowls.

"This isn't your goddamn smoke break! Do you even have the sword? If you're just trying to waste my time—"

"Dude," I say, cutting him off, "*Look*."

He pauses, his face still a mask of utter frustration. He lowers his gaze into the open needle book and freezes.

"That's..."

"Yup."

Tristan's mouth opens and closes a few times before any sound can escape. "Well—I—um—they must have shrunk it. Whoever took it, they must have shrunk it. I-I don't know why they would do that, but it doesn't matter now, because you found it, so I need it." Spindly, sheet-white fingers dart toward the sword.

"Hang on," I interrupt, pulling away. "So what you're saying is, it wasn't this small when you had it?"

"What? No, of course not, it's a sword. Just give—"

I skip backward, out of his reach. His face twists in confusion and anger.

"What are you—" He stops, and the deep furrows between his eyebrows smooth over. "Ah, right, the money." He shoves his hand into his jacket pocket and produces an envelope identical to the first that he gave me. The way he holds it out is casual enough to be dismissive. I shake my head.

"It's not about the money, Tristan. Who stole it?"

"What?" He looks at me like I've lost my mind.

"The chimeras couldn't have done it, they have *oven mitts* for hands. They had help. Who did it?"

The face-furrows return. Tristan's grip on the envelope tightens enough to irreparably dent the paper, and his jaw shifts as he grits his teeth. "How would I know? Just take the goddamn money and give me the sword, Matthew doesn't have much time—"

"Don't worry, he's not going to die in two days, remember? Give me a straight answer, Tristan."

Realization blooms across his face.

I pocket the needle case. "Yeah, no, I'm keeping this with me. I'll get it back to your family sometime, just not now. Not until I understand what's going on." I turn around and walk away, my gait light, keeping watch on Tristan out of the corner of my eye.

One... two... three... four footsteps before I hear the slide of gravel, a flicker of yellow light. Predictable bastard.

I spin with my arm outstretched, hand sweeping through the air to create a wake of distorted telekinetic energy. Tristan's spear of fire hits my shield head-on, splashing flames wide across its surface, then snuffing out. When both the fire and my shield have cleared, I see Tristan's stunned face, eyes wide like a goldfish's.

I take a running leap and tackle him.

We both hit the ground hard. Tristan doesn't make a very good cushion; he might be even bonier than I am. In a moment there's a shard in my hand, but I can't get it close to him with his arm tangled in mine. He manages to plant his other hand on my shoulder and shove—I lose my balance, thrown off sideways as he scrambles to his feet.

I get up just as quickly, with as much grace. He thrusts out his hand and another gout of fire speeds toward my face—I duck out of the way just in time. As the hair on the left side of my head singes, I dash forward and punch him in the face.

My fist glances off his jaw. Tristan yelps and staggers back against the alley wall, hands flying toward his face. When he tries to sink to the ground, I catch him by the lapels of his blazer and haul him back up.

"What the Hell did you get me into?" I demand. He blubbers in response—then tries to catch me by surprise with a punch to my injured cheek. I take it without letting go of his jacket—feel a half-second of explosive, neon nausea as his knuckles split open a scab—then slam him back against the wall. His head jerks like a ragdoll's, but he tenses and holds himself upright when I press a shard to the bottom of his jaw.

"Asking again. What the Hell is going on?"

Tristan's hands shake as they hover to either side of his head. His Adam's apple bobs as he swallows, eyes darting from side to side.

"I—I'm not—I'll tell you who hired me, just don't—"

His eyes fix on something just over my shoulder. Before I can react, my skull resounds with an impact so strong I feel it at the back of my eyes. One of my knees gives out first, and then the ground rushes up—

I'm on my back, listening to muffled voices. One is loud and panicked: Tristan's. The other is quiet, measured, borderline bored. I don't recognize it. I try my damnedest to open my eyes—oh, they're already open. That blackness is the sky. I try to get up, but the slightest movement sends a flash of searing agony through my skull, and I suck in a pained breath.

The voices stop. A shadow falls over me. The ground sticks to my back, forbidding me from getting up. Through my oddly clear vision, I see the silhouette of a bald man in a suit and sunglasses looming over me, the rubber sole of his boot rushing toward my face.

Quiet.

CHAPTER 5
A DAME WITH A MEAN BACKHAND

Someone slaps me awake. I can taste the magic behind the blow, and even before I open my eyes I'm ready for a fight. Well, not *quite* ready, given that I'm tied to a chair. Gods, my head hurts.

Squinting through the brain trauma and the stinging cheek, I'm able to focus on the face in front of me. Cheeks the gentle brown of autumn leaves, lips neatly tinted pink, mahogany eyes narrowed in anger. Looks kind of familiar, actually.

Holy shit.

"Miriam?" I croak.

"*Where is it?*"

Her voice is sharp enough to send another heavy throb through the back of my skull. I recoil, forgetting to answer the question.

"Miri, what—"

She flicks me in the forehead with a manicured finger. There's a colorful little *pop* at contact—an extra spark of the healing magic she used to wake me up the first time. The fuzz in my perception burns up like flash cotton, and suddenly I'm hyper-aware of the layered bruises on my face and the crisp edges of Miri's spoken syllables.

"Whatever you want to say to me right now, save it and answer the goddamn question. Where. Is. The. Sword?"

Sword. Right, there was a sword, that was important. Needle-sword, which I apparently don't have anymore, therefore...

"Tristan has it."

A collective groan goes around the room, and I finally notice that Miriam and I aren't alone. I'm in some kind of expensive lounge, big enough to accommodate the entire Meresti family, of which thirteen members are present. Behind me I hear the crackling of a fireplace, and in front of me a set of enormous, tightly-sealed double doors loom menacingly. An assortment of plush armchairs are arranged all around, yet the one chair I happen to be sitting in is rickety and made of uncomfortably solid wood. Figures. Also, my coat is missing.

Miri is standing with her hand to her head, squeezing her temples with a thumb and ring finger. Gods, she hasn't changed at all since I last saw her. She's still dressed in tastefully expensive business attire with her dreadlocks gathered up into a precise bun, she's still just an inch shorter than me in those sleek heels, and she's still utterly, undeniably beautiful. The only difference is the hostility in her stance, the way she's crossing an arm over her ribs to close herself off to me.

"I don't suppose," she says, painstakingly articulating each word, "that Tristan told you where he was going?"

My throat is dry. "I'm sorry, Miri."

"*Don't call me that,*" she hisses quietly.

"She's lying," a deep voice says, approaching from behind Miriam. It belongs to a massive hulk of a man with a wide, flat boxer's face, squeezed with difficulty into a three-piece suit. Said man is glaring at me in a vastly unfriendly manner. "You can't trust her."

"She's not lying," Miriam answers, eyes still on me. "Silas, stay out of this."

"She's *lying*," Silas insists. "She's working with Tristan and the Lockharts, we already know that. Of course she won't tell us the truth if we just *ask*." He balls his hand into a fist. I hear murmurs of agreement from some of the other Merestis, panicked dissent from others.

"If I needed you to play bad cop I would have told you," Miriam says, turning to face Silas while visibly resisting an eyeroll. "I know her, and she's not lying. Look, if you're so worried, make a truth charm."

"She got past our barriers, how do we know she

can't cheat a truth charm?"

Miriam grits her teeth. "She got through the barriers because *Tristan* was helping her behind the scenes, *not* because she's some kind of diabolical genius. Stop giving her more credit than she deserves."

"Wait," I interject, "Tristan lowered the barriers?"

"Of course he did," Miri says, waving me off in a *hush, the grown-ups are talking* kind of way. "How else could you have gotten to the sword?"

"Oh." There goes my I'm-a-special-ward-killer theory. Bummer.

"We don't have *time* for this!" Silas shouts to the ceiling. "The second Matthew dies this is all over! Pax is already in the infirmary—"

My head snaps up. "Wait, Pax? What happened to Pax?" I stare, wide-eyed, at Miriam. She sighs.

"My brother is sick."

"But—Dalia's punishment, it's not supposed to hit until after Matthew Meresti dies—right?"

She blows a puff of air out of her pursed lips. "It's not Dalia's anything, it's pneumonia. Magically induced. He lost a duel."

I deflate with relief, the corner of my lip twitching up. Good old Pax. You could challenge him to duel over a can of Pringles and he'd accept.

Miriam continues speaking. "From what we gather, when Dalia reclaims the life of an errant worshiper, you don't just lose years off your life: you age on the spot. Those of us under middle age still stand a pretty good chance of survival—but old age means a compromised immune system, and we all know how pneumonia and senior citizens get along. Pax will be sick for at least another month, and it's doubtful that our healers can keep Matthew alive for another week. We *need* that sword back."

My lip stops twitching. Silas is snarling audibly at me, his eyes as black as tar pits. Even his spiky hair seems to be bristling.

"Oh gods," I stutter. "Shit, I'm so sorry, I never meant to—"

"Don't give me that," Miriam says, cutting me off with a sharp, stern look. "I already know how sorry you are, and I don't want to hear it. I'm only interested in anything you can contribute to fixing this mess."

My tense shoulders drop. That... made me feel better than I thought it would. Sometimes Miriam's pragmatism can come off as cold, but other times it's a huge comfort to know someone's keeping it together better than you are.

Silas, on the other hand, is not keeping it together at all.

"She's playing you!" he shouts, getting right up in Miriam's face. The proximity doesn't go unnoticed; the entire room takes a synchronized step back. Even I dig my heels into the carpet and push back in my chair, attention captured by the way Miriam's eyes have narrowed into shadowed slits. She regards Silas with an unreadable steadfastness as his shouting rises in volume. He's somehow oblivious

to the way the tension in the room is thickening, building like water behind a dam. "All she has to do is look sad and sorry and you're already on her side! She should have been executed over a year ago, you know that—and you still trust her! You're betting everyone's lives on that trust! You're betting *Pax's* life on that trust! How can you be like this? She's playing you, and you're too wrapped up in whatever the Hell kind of—*fling* you used to have to see it!"

"ENOUGH."

Miriam's voice hangs in the air like the echo of bells in a cathedral, grinding the room to a halt. She stands with the power of a city behind her; at her command, twenty-two eyes burn holes into Silas's suit. Her sheer presence consumes and extinguishes Silas's the way a wildfire eats up a candle flame.

"Silas," she warns, upper lip curling, locking eyes without raising her chin an inch. "I know that marrying into this house has put a lot of pressure on you. I know that you are trying to show that you care, but this is *not* the way. You are either going to shut up or leave this room. Choose *now*."

Silas is rooted in place like a child staring into a furnace, feeling the heat on his brow and realizing just how *lucky* he is to be outside the steel walls. He still attempts to win back control, puffing up his chest to tower over Miriam's diminutive form. A second passes... Two. Three. Then his massive shoulders cave in, and he wordlessly turns and exits the room.

A short, awed silence. Then the Merestis remember who they are and get back to the immediate and crucial business of losing their heads. Voices rise in argument. An older member of the family pulls a still-smoldering Miriam away to badger her in urgent whispers. Some Merestis slump over in armchairs, heads in their hands in exasperated defeat. Others stormily pace alongside the walls where their ancestors' lavish portraits stare down in disapproval and disdain. I'm suddenly the most irrelevant person in the room. For all the attention I'm receiving, I may as well be a creaky extension of the chair I'm sitting in.

Miriam claps her hands, and the voices go silent.

"Gather everyone in the West Hall. Make sure we're not missing anyone."

Someone opens the door, prompting a crowd of eavesdropping apprentices on the other side to scatter like leaves. The thirteen mages filter out quickly, and I'm alone with my thoughts.

A clock over the fireplace mantle ticks with slow, heavy precision. My wrists ache where they've been lashed to the chair's wooden arms. Another rope has my shoulders pinned to the back of the chair, cutting through my shirt and into my deltoids. The Merestis even took the time to tie my ankles to the chair legs. Gods, my throat tastes like Elmer's glue. I tip my head back and close my eyes, grimacing as the throbbing pain within my skull shifts like an air bubble in a Magic 8 Ball. I flex my wrists under the rope, studying the ties; they're as elementary as shoelace knots. Tug on the right loop, and the whole thing will fall apart.

With some strategic shimmying, accompanied by a few deep-breathing exercises, I get the rope down over my chest so that it's slack at stomach-level. Now I can double over and get at the rope over my wrists with my teeth. Pull one loop, part of the knot comes undone. Find the right loop, pull again—

Something scuffs against the double doors from the other side. My head snaps up—oh fuck, ow, headache—and the world spins a full circle before my vision is restored. I hold my breath as the noise starts again. My first thought is that it's Silas, that either Miriam did order him to play bad cop or he's taken that responsibility upon himself. But the strange, frantic scrabbling doesn't seem human.

One of the doors cracks open, slowly. Something peeks through the bottom of the gap—a pink nose, fringed with tentacles. Every muscle in my body locks up in pure, unrelenting fear.

The chimera creeps in like the Grim Reaper's lesser-known cousin, leathery hide scraping against the doors as its wide body forces them open. I can't tell if it's more or less terrifying under the warm lights of the lounge than when it was lit only by my pathetic headlamp. Its legs are less stumpy and more agile than I remember; instead of waddling comically into the room, it slithers, belly rasping against the carpet, straight toward me.

I lurch forward and get the last bit of rope between my teeth, jerking it up and loose so I can wrestle my hand out of the opening. It takes some scraped skin and a slightly-dislocated thumb, but it works, and my right hand is finally free. I reach for the rope around my left wrist, fumbling with fat fingers at the knots. Fuck, the *one* time I need long nails—

The chimera is right in front of my feet now, its flat, oblong disc of a nose fluttering as its nostrils flare in my direction. It's unnerving, that face without eyes—it's judging you somehow, like the alabaster mask of a Greek chorus member.

The chimera *stands up on its hind legs*.

I slam backward in the chair, left hand still trapped and right hand gripping the chair's arm with bloodless knuckles. The chimera braces its front feet on my knees with its enormous claws, claws that can tear through concrete as easily as paper, extending toward me and grazing my thighs, ready to impale me with the most casual movement. It smells like damp graveyard dirt and the gutter. Its nose tentacles wriggle, straining toward me like pink worms. Oh gods. *This is how I die.*

"Shiny?"

Miriam's voice wafts in through the open doorway, accompanied by the clicking of heels. "Shiny, where did you go?"

The chimera's head swivels, but it doesn't budge from its position. Instead, both it and I watch Miriam poke her head into the room.

I almost burst into tears of relief. I shoot silent, telepathic pleas in Miriam's direction—*Help me, help me Miri, I'm really sorry please save me—*

Miriam's eyes light up. "There you are!"

What?

Miriam strolls into the room. "Shiny, what did I tell you about wandering around like that? Sharp is almost fully healed and he needs you right now."

"Shiny" makes a noise between a snort and a snuffle, nose tentacles wiggling in argument.

"I know he's asleep, but he'll be up soon." Miriam peers at me, acknowledging my presence for the first time since entering the room. "And he might be alarmed to find his sister smelling like the witch who nearly killed him."

My voice bubbles up into a confused, *"What?"*

Miriam comes over and affectionately pats Shiny's head. "Harry, this is Shiny. You stabbed her brother in the tunnels, remember? She's the one who raised the first alarm."

I stare at Shiny, and Shiny stares back. She has a trio of little black freckles on her nose, just below the left nostril; straining my gray matter, I can barely recall that the first chimera I ran into in the tunnels, the one that surprised me by bursting through the wall, had the exact same markings.

"Wait a second." I turn to Miriam. "These things are your pets?"

Shiny sends a blast of wet air flying at my face, forcing my eyes shut. Miriam shakes her head.

"Don't call them that, it's demeaning. The alligator moles are allies to the Merestis."

I'm about to express my shocked disbelief again,

but the pink tentacles waving in front of me like angry protest signs make me reconsider. "So... the sword was in the sewers because..."

"Because we entrusted it to our allies as a show of good faith, to solidify a tenuous alliance and to make reparations for past wrongs. The gator moles had qualms about touching a magical object and their teeth aren't made for handling delicate materials anyway, so we shrunk the sword down and put it in a protective bubble."

"Past wrongs? What kind of past wrongs?"

Shiny seems to have heard this history before, because she pushes off from my legs and waddles behind the chair to settle sleepily onto the carpet.

"We created them. Or rather, an ancestor did. But he rejected his creations and, well, disposed of them down the plumbing. A year or two ago, we ran into them again. Now we provide them with safe haven and food—food which, by the way, you burned down."

Shiny has no eyes but I'm still a hundred percent sure she's glaring at me.

"Food? What food? I didn't burn down any—" I stop short. "Oh. Tinkerbell."

Miriam's face screws up and she leans back, regarding me strangely. "Tinkerbell?"

"My fire sprite. That I just named Tinkerbell. You know, like the pissy little fairy from *Peter Pan*?"

Miri's brow shoots up, but settles in an instant. "Yes. Tinkerbell. Of course." I know she's being condescending, but I'm too happy about having named my sprite to care.

Miriam cocks her head and lowers her gaze to my wrist. "I came to let you go, but it looks like you've got that covered."

Oh, right. I hastily get back to untying my left wrist. Miriam's pointed gaze feels like a freeze ray, numbing my fingers and making the whole process fifty times harder than normal. I fumble for another minute before giving up and staring plaintively up at her.

Miriam drops her face into her hand. "Shiny?" she says, her voice muffled by the way she's grimacing into her palm, "Can you take care of these ropes?"

Shiny rouses herself and waddles back up to her previous position, using my legs as support again as she angles her snout to get at the rope. It shreds under her teeth like soft cheese, and she drops down to do the same with the bonds at my ankles.

"Thank you," I say, lifting the rope around my middle and simultaneously vowing never to get on a gator mole's bad side again. "I'm, um, really sorry about stabbing your brother. And burning down your food. And collapsing your tunnels."

The blank face stares at me, still accusing. Then Shiny tosses her snout and waddles out the door. I take a moment to be stunned by the blatant display of repto-mammalian sassery, then turn to Miriam.

"So, are you letting me go for old times' sake, or do you want something from me?"

Miriam crosses her arms. "Tristan paid you first,

but he forfeited all his known property rights when he broke his oath to us. That means you're on *our* payroll now. You're going after him."

My forehead wrinkles in surprise. "He's still in the city?"

Miriam gestures for me to stand up. I do, feeling my joints complain at the sudden spike in activity, and follow her out the door into the hallway.

"We dug up some of Tristan's old correspondences, found out he meant to sell the sword to the Lockharts and have them smuggle him out of the state." That makes sense. The Lockharts have been butting heads with the Merestis for centuries; theirs is a feud to rival the Cold War.

"I think I met one of their people. I had the sword and was trying to get the truth out of Tristan, but I got taken down by backup."

Miriam nods. "That was probably supposed to be the handoff, where the Lockharts got the sword and Tristan got the money and an easy escape. But something went wrong. The Lockharts didn't take the sword. They should be blackmailing us by now—or gloating, at the very least—but instead they're refusing association with Tristan and have withdrawn entirely from the matter. They sent a messenger right to our front door. Cocky bastards."

I remember Tristan and the bald mystery thug arguing. "What do you think happened?" I ask, eyes occupied by the opulent velvet wallpaper and intricately paneled doors as we move through the hall. Much like Miriam, the Merestis' mansion hasn't changed at all.

"I have no idea. But whatever it was, it gave us time to scrub Tristan's room and use the DNA to put up a specified blood perimeter around the city—thank the Goddess we even managed that, the motion was almost struck down by a collective senior referendum."

"Collective senior what?"

"Never mind, it's a family thing. The point is, Tristan is somewhere within the five boroughs, and he's trapped."

I squint at the back of Miriam's head. "Okay, so what do you need me for? It looks like you've got everything covered. Just send out your people to track him down. If you scare him enough he might even do the pigeon-flying-into-a-glass-window thing against the perimeter." Boy, I'd pay to see that.

Miriam sighs heavily. "I wish. The sword is Tristan's best leverage. As long as there's even a chance of his destroying it, we can't risk spooking him." Her lip curls into a scowl. "Or at least, that's what the seniors keep insisting. Cowards. I've mobilized most of our more discreet assets to keep an eye out, but until there's a proper majority ruling I can't have them *do* anything."

"But if Tristan destroys the sword, isn't he ruining himself too?"

"Not quite. Stairs." We turn into a spiral stairwell and begin making our way down. "Dalia added another condition to her deal with Matthew. It says that if he breaks the contract, his people will suffer to the degree in which they've already benefited from her boon. Tristan has been an official member of the family for barely a month. If he destroys the sword, the blowback will be much less severe for him than for the rest of us. He might develop some wrinkles, an inconvenient bald patch or two. But for those of us who've been beholden to Dalia since grade school…"

I may not survive this. I understand the words, even if she doesn't say them out loud. I chew the inside of my cheek as we exit the stairwell into another hallway, this one with plainer, rougher walls.

"So Tristan's hunkered down in a safehouse somewhere, and your people can't go near him. You need him found by someone who won't scare him too much, at least not enough to make him destroy the sword. For instance, someone he recently got the better of." I reach up to rub the aching bruise at the back of my head, and the faded bootprint on my face throbs in tandem. "Sound logic. What'd the rest of the board say?"

"Nothing. This is an executive decision."

"You *do* make a lot of those," I mumble under my breath.

She stops short, forcing me to do the same. As my shoes skid on the hard floor, she turns to face me partially, glaring from the corner of her eye. I have to fight not to flinch. When she speaks, every syllable is laced with barbed wire.

"I make these decisions because I have to, for the

sake of my family. And I'm damn good at it. It's the entire reason my family adopted me, and it's how I repay them for the years past. I have good reasons for the choices I make. Care to say the same?"

I'm paralyzed from the neck down. I can't meet her eyes. "...Sorry," I mutter. She glares for a moment longer, then resumes walking at a brisk pace, forcing me to catch up. "You, uh, have any leads on where Tristan might be?"

"We have one. The whole time he was living with us, Tristan was intensely paranoid about his privacy. He took every opportunity possible to leave the mansion, and when he came back he always refused to tell us where he'd been. We were concerned, naturally. We put a tail on him and identified one of the addresses he frequented."

I decide to let slide the flippant admittance to familial stalking in favor of getting more information. "Okay, so what is it? Warehouse? Safehouse?"

"Sex dungeon."

"...Oh."

"There's a reason we never confronted him about it."

"Good call." The lights are getting dimmer and the air is clammier, colder. "Where are we going?"

"To get your coat. Here." She stops at a door marked with circular sigils, ones of binding and suppression, insulation. Miriam presses her wrist against a panel on the door. It opens, and we enter.

It's a laboratory of some sort. The walls are

occupied by shelves, which are in turn lined with rows and rows of materials I'd have to sell a kidney to get ahold of: herbs, jewels, fluids extracted from exotic animals, corrosive chemicals, and, of course, vials and vials of blood. Against the white, sterile walls, the cobalt blue of Miriam's skirt suit stands out like a beacon.

I spot my coat spread out across the length of a silver table. A white-haired, white-robed technician is extracting and examining the contents in its pockets.

"Murdoch," Miriam says, "We already told you, the sword's not in there. You can stop searching now."

"I know, I know," Murdoch says with a thick Irish accent, refusing to look up from her work. "There's just so many damn *pockets*. I've found two more in the last ten minutes, and there's something else—here, inside the seam—but I can't tell how to get to it—"

"That's probably the candy bars," I offer helpfully, tiptoeing to make myself seen over Miriam's head.

"Candy bars?" Murdoch whips her head toward me, shaggy bob bouncing around her temples, eyes bleary behind oversized goggles.

"Yeah, here." I stride over, worm my hand into a hidden opening, and pull out a Twix bar. "See?"

Murdoch stares. She throws up her hands.

"A candy bar. Of course it's a fokkin' candy bar." She storms out of the room, still muttering to herself.

I get to work replacing the contents of my coat, each item to its rightful pocket.

As I move, I become aware of the eerie silence behind me. Miriam is still there; every once in a while there's the click of a heel against the polished floor, a discreet cough. I keep expecting her to address me again, to say—anything. But even when I've reclaimed the last of my belongings, she's mute.

I turn as I shrug on my coat and see Miriam's face as impassive as stone. "Come here," she says, her voice betraying no shred of emotion. I obey. She reaches up for my cheek, and I finally remember how scraped up my face is. The cut I got from the gator mole tunnels is scabbed over again under the twisted, sticky Band-Aid, smarting and covered in grime just like the rest of my injuries. Miriam delicately peels the corner of the Band-Aid off, and I wince at the way it tugs at my skin.

"I'm going to take the whole thing off," she says without looking into my eyes. "Ready?"

I nod. I react with nothing but a silent clenching of my teeth as she rips off the adhesive, leaving behind sticky skin and a crusty scab. She brushes the wound lightly with a knuckle, letting sparks of magic jump from her fingertips to my skin, dissolving the scab in a matter of seconds and rearranging its molecules to provide a layer of clean, unbroken flesh.

"You have one on your ankle too, right?"

"Uh, yeah."

I wrestle off my boot and sock and hop onto the

table, feeling like a particularly large lab rat. I hope my feet don't smell too bad. Instead of undoing the bandages around my ankle, Miriam simply pushes her magic through them and into the torn muscle. I sigh quietly in relief.

"Thanks," I say, hopping back onto the floor, bending to put my shoe and sock back on. She doesn't move an inch as I do, and I'm forced to stare at the pointed toes of her heels the whole time I'm bent over, struggling to tie my laces. Gods, what is with me and knots today? I do a shabby job but stand up anyway, hoping the awkwardness will leave once I can see Miriam's face again.

She catches me entirely by surprise. Her stone look is gone. She's not angry either; there's no trace of the earlier ire she directed at Silas. Instead there's something… hurt. Worried. Mournful. Like she has something important to ask me, and she already knows it's going to kill us both inside.

"Miriam?" I say, quietly.

"Why didn't you tell me as soon as Tristan came to you?" Miriam's voice is so soft I can barely hear it. "You knew from the beginning that this was my family on the line. You of all people should know how much that means to me. Even if you believed Tristan's story, I had a right to know someone was going behind my back to put my people in danger. But you took the money and the deal, and you never even planned to tell me. Why?"

I can feel the blood drain from my face. "I—I—" I don't know how to explain it to her. I never *meant* to hurt her, I wasn't taking Tristan's side over hers, I was just—just— "I thought you didn't want to see me."

Miriam's brow wrinkles in confusion. "What? You risked your life, my family's lives, Pax's life, my life—because you thought I didn't want to *see* you?"

"I know it sounds bad when you say it that way, but the flowers, and the card—"

Realization dawns across Miriam's face, smoothing out the creases...then ironing them back in, more deeply than before. "*That's* what you're angry about? *That's* why you did this?"

My gut is roiling with something I hadn't even realized was there, an emotion that hasn't had an outlet for a good fourteen months. The levee breaks; the river overflows.

"Miri, you *promised* you would be there for me! But then the second something came up, you *ran!*"

I see it in Miri's face too: a crack in the furnace door, steel giving way, orange flames furling out to meet me head-on. "That 'something' was a failed demon blood spell and an excommunication! There are limits to what you can expect from your friends!"

"But you just *had* to leave me hanging—'Don't try to contact me, I'll call you as soon as my family gets off my back'—you wrote it on a pretty little card and stuck it on a basket of yellow tulips and had it sent right to my hospital room. And I waited, and I kept waiting, and all that time I had no idea you'd already given up on me!"

"Look, things were difficult, alright? You

wouldn't understand, since you apparently don't care enough about your friends to spare them from your own stupidity!"

"What's *that* supposed to mean?"

"I told you I would be there for you because I thought I would be. Because I thought I *could* be. Because I never once imagined you would be so callous as to force me to choose between my family and you! I trusted you not to do that to me, and you broke that trust the second you picked up that syringe!"

I feel a sharp, pinching pain at the side of my neck, right at the center of my scar; my arm twitches with the urge to slap it off my skin. Instead, I bite down on the inside of my cheek hard enough to draw blood.

"That had *nothing* to do with you," I grit out, tasting copper.

Miriam notices my reaction—she must have—and stands her ground. "Like *Hell* it did. It affected me, didn't it? Did you ever consider what it was like, being close to you when it all came crashing down? How terrifying it was to be dragged into court and cross-examined for reasons to lop off your head? How much of my family's trust and goodwill I lost just by association, in less than a fucking day?" She sweeps her hand out toward the door. "You saw that in the lounge just now with Silas. How much worse do you think it was back then?"

My scar still stings. It's like the pain is draining my ability to speak.

Miriam stalks closer. "Did you ever take the time to think of the consequences your actions had on anyone other than yourself? Or were you too busy blaming the only friend you had left for your misery?"

Her face is inches from mine now. With a jolt, I realize there are bags under her eyes that I couldn't see before, not from far away with all those layers of concealer on top. Are those fine lines etched across her face, or just a trick of the light?

The tone of Miriam's voice dips dangerously low. Her mahogany eyes never once leave mine. "You screwed me over once before, Harry. You have no idea how much blood and sweat and humility and fucking *patience* it took for me to get back in the position I'm in now. This is where I should have been over a year ago, where I need to be to protect this fucked up, dysfunctional family from itself—to protect it from people like Tristan, and from people like *you*. I swear to Dalia, if your immaturity is what costs me my people, I will hurt you in ways even the demon blood couldn't."

Blood roars in my ears. I barely register Miriam pulling a pen and notepad out of her jacket pockets, scribbling something, ripping the sheet out of the pad and shoving it into my hand.

"The address of the dungeon, and a number to call once you have the sword. You can escort yourself out."

All the possible things I could say are jumbling up in my head, piling on top of each other, creating a buzzing chaos—*I'm sorry—I didn't know—I never meant to*—then the door to the laboratory slams shut, and I'm alone.

I sink to the floor with my back against a steel table leg, clutching the creased paper in my hand. She's right. Miriam is right. In fourteen months I never once considered the toll my sentence would've had on her. On anyone, really. If I'd realized I might have acted differently, but I never realized, because I didn't *think*. All I did was sit and stew in my own bitterness until I convinced myself that I was somehow the victim in all of this.

I draw my knees closer and drop my face into them. The freezing cold of the floor seeps through my pants and into my skin. The faint smell of decay hangs in the air, buoyed up by the less-faint smell of formaldehyde. And then there's dull magic humming below the surface of it all, lethargic as any preserved specimen, stale as the shame stopping up my throat.

…No. It doesn't matter how I feel right now. The mess Miriam's family is in is my fault, so it's my job to fix it. The table leg digs into my spine as I push up off the floor. I take a step, then another, and another. And I leave this pit of dead, stagnant flesh behind.

The second I reach the hallway, it occurs to me that I don't know my way around the Merestis' mansion. As much as I'd love to be out of here, I don't know where the exit is, and there are no convenient green-lit signs pointing it out. I manage to recall Miriam's earlier route enough to find and climb the spiral staircase, but once I'm a floor up I'm truly lost. Shit. Should I knock on a few doors, see if anyone's around to give directions?

Something hard and scaly pokes the back of my ankle. I skip forward out of shock, then turn to see Shiny on the floor behind me, snout tilted upward in greeting.

"Oh," I say, blinking at her. "Hello."

Shiny snuffles at me.

"Are you... here to show me the way out?"

Shiny nods an affirmative, snout almost banging into the floor with the force of the gesture. She waddles past me, tapping my leg with her tail as a motion to follow.

She takes me down the hallway to a set of stairs I hadn't noticed before, then starts climbing up. She places her feet carefully and uses her scaly belly like a surfboard, propelling it up the steps with her stumpy legs. It's an adorable sight, and it cheers me up a whole lot. I follow her as diligently and politely as I can.

Another hallway, through a lounge, more rows of doors. How many rooms does this damn mansion have?

Then I hear hushed voices just ahead, coming from inside an open door. Shiny seems ready to slither right past and so am I, until I identify one of the voices as Miriam's. I creep quietly to the doorway and peer in.

It's a study with all the lights off. The only source of illumination is the window, which is covered by a curtain too thin to conceal the approaching dawn. In the bluish shadows I see the outline of Miriam's figure, as well as that which is unmistakably Silas's.

They're speaking too quietly for me to hear what they're saying. Silas's earlier restless agitation seems to have subsided; his head is bowed and he's unmoving, an exhausted stone giant. Miriam's tone is reassuring, comforting. She strains up toward him, her whole body following the motion. And then she gently, gently clasps his hand in both of hers.

I know that marrying into this family has put a lot of pressure on you...

I swallow. Miriam isn't wearing any rings, but then again, neither is Silas. I don't know what to do with this information. It shouldn't matter to me. Why should it matter to me? It's not some kind of betrayal—sure, I had a crush on her when we were nineteen, but it only took one kiss for that to fizzle out on both our ends. Mostly. And it's not like you're required to tell your friends that you've tied the knot, especially if said "friends" just jeopardized the lives and safety of your entire family. But... is it wrong of me to feel just a little sad?

A light tug at my pants leg. I look down to see Shiny holding the fabric of my slacks delicately in her mouth, pulling me forward with impatient movements.

"Okay," I say, softly, so as not to alert Miriam and Silas. "Okay, I'm coming." I move away from the door, ready to follow Shiny again, and the chimera lets out a satisfied snuffle before continuing on her way.

I don't even pay attention to the rest of the mansion. Before I know it, Shiny has led me to the antechamber in front of the building's thick double doors.

"Thank you," I say, nodding respectfully toward her. She huffs air out of her wet nose. I dawdle a bit, chewing my lip, trying to think of an eloquent apology for last night.

"...Here," I say, fishing three candy bars out of my coat. Shiny's snout lifts in interest. "I'm sorry, I know I owe you guys a lot more, but this is what I have right now. I'll make up for the rest soon, I promise."

For a moment, it seems like Shiny's going to hautily refuse the offer. Then she stretches upward and snaps the aluminum-covered packets out of my hand. I can't help but smile.

"Thank you for the second chance."

Shiny is too busy waddling away to respond, prizes held tightly in her vise-like jaw. I watch her for a moment, then turn and leave the building.

CHAPTER 6
A DAME WITH A MEANER BACKHAND

The dungeon is tucked into a snug, spacious suite above a nail salon in Midtown. Given different circumstances, I might have wandered in here on my own. The nondescript door is soaked through with sexual energy, like a perfumed handkerchief — but, unlike perfume, the magic nuzzles up against my skin and invites me forward with fleeting, yet insistent touches. I let it guide me to the doorbell, then push with a firm fingertip.

I rub the corners of my eyes as I wait for a response. I'm a little groggy, having passed the last few hours of the early morning napping in my apartment. I wish I'd dreamed; maybe then the nap wouldn't have felt so short.

Actually, scratch that. No dreams is better than bad dreams.

Someone finally buzzes me in. The door swings open just a moment after, courtesy of a tanned brunette with smoky, heavy-lidded eyes and lips as red as her rubber corset. "*Welcome* to The Jezebel's Lair," she lilts. "Do you have an appointment?"

I shake my head. Her chuckle is low but perfectly clear, like a seamless stage whisper. She beckons coyly for me to follow her inside, and I do.

"I am Vivienne," she says as she sways down the short hallway, lights shimmering in kaleidoscope patterns off her glossy boots, "but that'll be 'Madame Vivienne' to you." I give a quiet nod in the affirmative, and she doesn't press me further. Presently, we arrive at a lobby, nicely furnished with ornate rugs, gilt-framed mirrors, and Renaissance-style depictions of tortured men hung along the walls. I wrinkle my nose at the saggy male buttocks, and Vivienne smiles sympathetically. "Apologies for the view, we usually cater to a different clientele."

"No worries, just reminding myself to do my squats."

She laughs loudly at that, then gestures toward a nice, solidly supportive vintage armchair. "Make yourself comfortable." I settle down, and echoes of jittery emotion jump up from the cushions to prick me in the back. Vivienne remains standing before me, relaxed with a hip thrust to one side. "Since you haven't made an appointment with a specific domme, we'll do a meet with those available right now. Any requests?"

Things are about to get tricky. Since places like this don't appreciate threats to their clients' anonymity, I doubt it'll go over well if I ask for "the one that Tristan Meresti gets his skinny white ass beaten by." I could just go with the meet, try to guess which of the women presented would most appeal to a trust fund baby with a traitorous streak, but I don't have much faith in that plan. The person I'm looking for may not even be in the building right now. I'm still stalling, trying to come up with a way to break the delicate situation to Vivienne, when one of the doors to the lobby opens and a succubus steps in.

She's thin, white, and made entirely of harsh, symmetric angles, an impression heightened by the way her latex catsuit hugs her knife-sharp hipbones. She's also *ridiculously* tall by merit of her enormous, heeled boots. Her bleach blond hair is pulled back into an unforgiving ponytail, revealing a beauty spot on her left cheekbone and unnaturally long, soot-black eyelashes.

She recognizes my nature by the way I recognize hers. Her thin, painted lips curl into a smile, and her hips roll as she turns to approach me.

Vivienne notices my shift in interest and turns around just in time for the latex-clad figure to reach us. "Thank you, Viv," the succubus says, her voice seeming to reach out and brush against my cheek.

"I'll take it from here." Vivienne doesn't question how the succubus and I know each other. She simply smiles, nods, and disappears down the corridor.

The succubus orders me to stand with the crook of a finger. I'm on my feet in an instant. "So," she says in a voice like heavy, twisting silk, smiling down at me—gods, I do appreciate the chance to look up at a woman—"What brings you here, blood mage?"

I put my hands in my pockets with an apologetic shrug. "Politics, unfortunately." Damn, I hate to waste a good conversation like this. "The internal affairs kind."

She raises a perfectly penciled eyebrow. "I thought the witch with the demon blood scar didn't do politics?"

I let loose a heavy sigh. "You have no idea how much I wish that were true."

She chuckles low, making my stomach flutter. "I'm Laylah—Mistress Laylah, if you were really here as a client." She raises her eyes, which are blue as Chinese porcelain, to a security camera dutifully camped up in the corner of the ceiling. She beckons for me to follow, back into the hallway she just emerged from, then into one of the rooms.

The whole room is awash with scarlet, so much so that the color reflects off both her and my skin. There's a fancy four-poster bed, its pitch black frame dangling with chains and cuffs, as well as a St. Andrew's cross propped up against a corner. Torture implements are neatly organized on a rack built into the wall. The faint smell of disinfectant lingers in the air.

"Just had a client?" I ask, stepping around a spanking bench.

"Over half an hour ago. Took a while to clean up though, and it doesn't help that there's no windows in here."

She turns around to face me, and suddenly something is off. Eyes, it's her eyes—they're darkening, desaturating to a warm gray, then fading into deep brown. Mahogany.

Laylah sees me balk at her new appearance and smirks. "Someone on your mind?" she purrs. Her pale skin is quickly tanning to autumn brown.

I cough, trying to keep my voice from cracking. The pink of my cheeks isn't just due to the walls. "No offense, just, uh, I would really prefer you didn't do that. I know it's natural, a-and I know you're only imitating what's in my head, but, um, she and I have—history. She's also kinda-sorta my boss right now. And she's, uh, married."

"Ah, I understand." I expect her to shift back into her previous form—instead, she flashes a grin full of sharp ivory canines, her hair tightening into thick, black curls. Demon curls. Godsdammit.

"Can we *please* go back to the blond porn star fantasy?" I say, trying and failing to shield my eyes with a cupped hand. Both her skin and hair bleach to their original shades, her facial features elongating and sharpening like hand-pulled glass. I breathe a sigh of relief. "Thank you."

"More than one woman on your mind, I take it?" The smirk still hasn't left her face.

"That's... not important right now. I'm here about an apprentice mage. Blue eyes, black hair, pale beyond reason. Stick-skinny, nervous wreck, probably dressed like a prep schooler. Have you seen him?"

She tilts her head to one side, making her ponytail sway behind her. "I have, actually. He's a regular. Not one of mine, but I do know who sees him, and I can tell you where she is. For a price, obviously."

I dip my head in acknowledgment. "Obviously."

She reaches for my collar. I stiffen immediately, but will myself to relax as she tugs my neckline down and runs a fingertip lightly across my damaged skin. It barely tickles.

"Your magic is corrupted," she murmurs, eyes fixed on my scar. "I want to know how that tastes."

I keep my chin up, feeling my pulse speed up and hoping she can't feel it under the scar tissue. "I thought sex was illegal here?"

"It is. Anything that involves penetration or exchange of bodily fluids, anyhow. But that doesn't matter. I'm celibate." She abruptly stops touching me and moves away. I blink after her.

"Wait, you're celibate?"

"Have been for years." She reaches a large wheel in the corner. "The deed itself is too messy for my taste. This job allows me to forego it entirely while remaining comfortably fed. Not to mention, I always did have an affinity for this..." She waves her gloved hand vaguely at the room. "...flavor."

She grasps a handle protruding from the side of the wheel and starts to turn it. There's a rattle of chains from above; I follow it with my eyes to see a set of metal and leather cuffs descending from the ceiling. When I catch Laylah's gaze again, there's a knowing gleam in her eye.

"Now, tell me sweetheart—are you a masochist?"

***

"Are you a masochist?"

The question takes me off guard. I look up from the bookshelf, where a heavy volume remains half-extracted, teetering on the brink of a long fall.

"Uh, yeah, I think. A bit." *Why do you ask? The words are on the tip of my tongue, but I hold them back. Johanna will explain, she always does.*

"That's good. Come here."

She walks—no, glides toward her desk, silk robe billowing out behind her in a wave of liquid rose gold. Light streams in from the floor-to-ceiling windows behind her and refract around her form, turning her into a tall and winding silhouette. She puts something down on the desk's surface and beckons me over. I shove the precarious book back onto the shelf and skip lightly across the wooden floor on my bare feet.

"Everything is energy," Johanna says, her unique mixture of accents—Northern Indian being the most prominent—making her voice dip and weave through the

air like a fluttering ribbon. I drink in every word. "Everything a witch does is reliant upon harnessing energy. Pain is energy also, albeit in a more abstract form, and the simplest, most visible expression of energy is light. Now, I normally wouldn't resort to toys, but given your distinct lack of elemental ability..."

I bite my lip, but not before she catches my apologetic simper. "I'm really sorry about the curtains." A few sad scraps of said curtains still hang above the window, charred at the edges.

Johanna glances up at me, then at the destroyed drapes. I catch a smile in her murky gray eyes. "They needed replacing anyhow. Now, watch."

The gadget on the desk is nothing more than a lightbulb the size of my thumbnail with two wires extending out of its sides, making the whole structure look like a futuristic laurel wreath. Johanna rolls up her sleeves and forms a 'V' with the index and ring fingers of her left hand, then presses the pad of each finger against the exposed ends of wire. With her free hand, she picks up a sewing pin and jabs it into the back of her hand.

The lightbulb flares to life. I hold my breath as it glows steadily for one... two... three... four seconds, before fading to darkness once again. Johanna takes her fingers off the wires and hands me the pin.

"Try it."

I place my fingers exactly as she did, wielding the pin like a tiny sword as I muster my concentration. Then I clench my teeth and drive it into the back of my hand.

No light. The pin sticks straight up out of my skin between my third and fourth knuckles, like a flag on the moon. I pull it out and stab myself again, this time harder—the lightbulb remains depressingly unresponsive. As a droplet of blood wells up from the first puncture, I look helplessly up at Johanna. She shakes her head.

"I'll tell you what you did wrong. You tensed. You tried to save yourself from the pain. It's a natural human reaction, one I understand completely, but for this lesson it is an obstacle. You have to feel the pain. You have to see it through, or else its power is useless. Here."

She opens a desk drawer and extracts a case of small, flat razor blades. She takes my hand off the device, plucks out the pin, and heals the tiny puncture wounds with a quick pass of her fingers. Her hands are heavy and warm and slightly calloused, lighter and pinker at the palm than the rest of her ochre brown skin; I'll never get tired of feeling them against mine. She holds my hand palm-up and presses the edge of a blade against it.

"Don't worry about the magic just yet. Just feel. And don't try to hold anything in; stoicism has no place here. Blood mages are volatile and emotional, and our strength comes from translating that restlessness into power. Do that now."

She slides the blade against my skin. It stings immediately, furiously, crimson blood rushing to the surface. My first instinct is to hold my breath, squeeze my eyes shut, and clench every muscle that isn't in my right hand.

Johanna's voice drifts slowly to my ears, as though from a distance.

"Remember, don't hold back."

I release the stale breath from my lungs and the tension from my muscles. I open my eyes and watch the blade's progress across my skin. The more flesh Johanna opens up, the louder the pain—my voice shakes as it escapes my throat as a whimper.

But I keep looking. I keep feeling. Somewhere in all that white-hot, searing, screaming sensation is a flicker of something tangible. Something I can use.

Johanna stops cutting. The wound is maybe about two inches long, bleeding profusely, and I feel the entire length of it. I accept it, let it crackle through my veins as a current, and pick up the two ends of the wire.

The bulb flickers on, shakily, more like a candle buffeted by wind than any reliable technological invention. But it doesn't matter. I did it. I don't even realize I'm grinning until my cheeks ache.

"Good job," Johanna says, eyes crinkling at the edges as the corners of her lips quirk up. I'm mesmerized by the guttering light, trying to will it stronger. But Johanna gently takes ahold of my wrist, and I reluctantly abandon the wires to let her heal the cut on my hand.

"Now, a disclaimer," she says, wiping blood off my palm with a handkerchief.

I stick my tongue out and blow a raspberry. "Shouldn't you have done the disclaiming **before** *the risk was taken?"*

"You wouldn't have understood what I was saying before. Harnessing pain means feeling it, as you just saw. If you continue turning to pain as a method of generating power—which, by the gleam in your eye, I suspect you will—you'll become used to opening up and accepting

harm that comes your way.

"In other words, you'll make yourself vulnerable. And if one day you are hurt, severely, you will lack the defenses most people have against physical, mental, and emotional trauma. Your only solution will be to wait out the suffering, see it through to the end, and hopefully pick up the pieces. It may consume you, at least temporarily. It may scar you permanently. But that is the price a blood witch pays."

I listen to her as attentively as I can, but in the back of my mind I know I'll never truly understand what she's saying until I run into the problem myself. All I can really do is file the advice away and hope I'm smart enough to remember it when the time comes.

A thought occurs to me.

"What does this have to do with me being a masochist again?"

"Oh, that. I've already told you I can't teach you much about sex magic—it's simply not what I'm proficient at—but I can teach you this. Pleasure and pain are two sides of a very thin coin. I've just shown you one side, and I'm sure that with some experimentation, you can discern the other for yourself."

"So, what, you're telling me to go get beaten up by a hot girl?"

She arches an eyebrow, her mouth twitching into a half-smirk.

***

I dangle from the ceiling by my wrists at the center of the room, completely naked but for my boxers. Each wrist is cuffed and chained to the ends of a metal rod that Laylah is drawing up to the ceiling via pulley. I'm standing on the balls of my feet, not quite tiptoeing, but still struggling to find purchase on the floor. Gravity thins and stretches out my frame. I'm certain that if Laylah were to leave me like this without laying a single hand on my body, I'd be sore all over in twenty minutes.

Heavy heels *clop clop* on the floor as Laylah approaches from behind. She flips my ponytail over my shoulder, and the briefest touch of latex against my bare skin makes me shiver. She notices instantly, chuckling as she toys with the little hairs at the nape of my neck.

"When was the last time you did this?" she says.

"It's... been a while," I admit. "I might take some time to warm up."

"Well, lucky for you. I happen to have a good—" she checks a clock somewhere nearby, "—hour and a half to kill before my next appointment."

I hear the slap of soft leather strips against rubber gloves; it's like an auditory aphrodisiac. My entire body stands to attention, skin thrumming in anticipation.

"Safeword?" she asks.

"Butterfly."

She hums. "Interesting choice."

And then she waits. The sound of my own breathing grows loud in my ears. I'm on the verge of an inhale when she hits me.

I rock forward purely out of surprise, sucking in

a small breath. The noise is bigger than the impact, but I definitely feel it—loose impact, a momentary nip from the sharper tips of the flogger's tails, then the slide of soft, heavy leather strips down my back. Like teeth, then a full-lipped kiss. She hits me again, a little harder. Then again. And again. The layered stinging melts across my skin, warming it, making it more sensitive and responsive.

As the strikes get harder I hear my voice starting to escape with each breath. Her pace is slowing but she's putting her wrist into every lash, forcing the skin-deep pain to take root in deeper muscle. I resist the urge to tense the muscles in my back, instead wrapping my hands loosely around the chains at my wrists and dropping my head, feet flexing. The space between each hit is an exercise in anticipation. I count my breaths to match.

Back to the quicker, more lenient strikes. One, two, three, four lashes, alternating diagonal strikes creating an 'X' on my back—and then a hard, punishing *THWAP!*

The chains jingle as I straighten up in surprise, a little "*Mmm,*" coming from between my closed lips. Oh, I get it, new pattern. The four softer, regular strikes wind me up, preparing me—then the fifth I feel like a lightning bolt through my entire body. I squirm when it hits, thighs tightening, whining under my breath. I sink into the rhythm, all thoughts in my mind trickling out like hourglass sand, replaced by a mantra of *one, two, three, four, five... one, two, three, four, five...*

She's merciful, for a bit. As my eyes close and my limbs relax, she lets me enjoy the regularity for about a minute longer. Then she follows up a fourth hit with a pause. Before the lack of sensation can shake me from my daze, she belts me with a heavy leather strap.

The unfamiliar *THUD* wakes me immediately, making me yelp and arch my back. Just to make sure I'm really paying attention, Laylah gives the outsides of my thighs each a heavy slap; I skip from side to side, clumsily stepping on my own toes. She laughs, the sound a cascade of silver bells.

"Getting a little too comfortable, are we?" she says, "I can smell it."

It takes me a second to realize my boxer briefs are soaked between my thighs. A bit of blood rushes to my face, and my knees knock together.

Then a gloved fingertip draws up the length of my spine. I let out a shuddering gasp, muscles in my back going rigid as her touch sends my frayed nerves into overdrive.

"You said it had been a while since you'd done this," she muses, "Any reason for that?"

"I—took a break," I gasp, "Wasn't in a good place—*ahh*—mentally."

"I assume you've recovered at this point?"

My muscles twitch and spasm in the wake of her touch. It's taking all of my will just to keep from writhing shamelessly where I stand. "Y-yeah. Took a few months, but I got my shit sorted."

She gives a small hum of approval. "That's a

lovely thing to hear. The profanity, less so. Watch your tongue or I'll clamp it with chopsticks."

She steps back and hits me with the strap again, making a *"Yes-ma'am-sorry-ma'am-won't-happen-again-ma'am"* tumble from my lips.

"Oh, and I prefer 'mistress.' 'Ma'am' makes me sound old."

I squint at the ceiling. "Aren't you immortal?"

THUD.

I moan, squeezing my eyes shut, calves burning as I rise on my toes to clutch the chains in my hands. Okay, maybe I deserved that one.

Laylah's boots *clop clop* again as she drifts away, probably looking for some other toy. I take advantage of the short break she's given me, swallowing to wet my dry throat, shifting my feet to get as much traction on the floor as possible. A slight sheen of sweat is making my hair stick to my neck and shoulder. As Laylah's footsteps return, my heartbeat quickens of its own accord.

She swings the toy in her hand, and I hear it cut through the air with a menacing whistle. I gulp.

"That sounds... not nice."

I can *feel* her smirk. "Darling, *I'm* not nice."

She swings again—thin, hard, knotted strands cut into my back. It feels like trails of needles sticking into my skin. The pinching, burning pain is shallow but lasting, and I find myself whimpering pathetically as I squirm. Two more strikes, and hot tears well up in my eyes. I can't help but dance on my toes, wanting to soothe the pain so badly but finding no possible escape.

"You don't like this one, do you?" Laylah hums, a note of amusement coloring her voice.

I scream as she unleashes the next dozen blows as a rapid flurry—needles, needles, fire, ow ow ow—and I hear her giggle like a schoolgirl in response. The sound goes straight to my head, making me cross one of my legs over the other and squeeze tight, panting with my teeth clenched.

"Legs. Open."

I try, I really try, but my muscles have locked into place. My arms ache. All of my weight is being supported by my poor wrists, but I'm not in control enough to fix the problem.

…A second later, a rubber strap as wide as her hand and as thick as a doorstop THUMPs into my back. The air *oophs* out of my lungs as the impact jars my entire frame—it's like a hard reset, forcing me to slump back into my original position and focus all my attention on regaining my breath. The leather strap Laylah used on me before was a slap bracelet compared to this one's kangaroo punch. Funnily enough, I've stopped crying. It's like the strap knocked the tears right out of me.

"Th-thank you, Mistress," I wheeze.

"Mmm, no need. I've been waiting to use that one. Two more, darling."

THUMP.

THUMP.

I sag against the chains, groaning. The stinging tattoo of shallow pain on my back is mostly gone, replaced by a bone-deep ache. The abused skin on my back is radiating enough feverish warmth to counteract a New England blizzard, and every joint from my wrists to my shoulders is screaming. I'm glad I'm not wearing pants, because the cling of sweat-soaked fabric against my inflamed skin would probably kill me right now. I'm too out of sorts to do anything but shiver, eyes briefly rolling back, as Laylah grazes her fingers down the outsides of my arms, then the sides of my ribs.

"One more round and you'll be *perfect* to eat," she purrs.

I twist my head weakly in her direction, licking my dry lips. The room is a red liquid haze that seeps into my mouth to slur my words. "Speaking of eating, what do you think I'll taste like? I'm thinking maybe a nice, big platter of *whipped cream*. Ha, get it? Whipped—"

CRACK!

The tip of the four-foot-long bullwhip barely misses me, cracking the air just to my left. I stiffen anyway, back straightening like a flagpole and eyes snapping open. Laylah chuckles behind my shoulder.

"Whipped cream. Hah, that's funny. I'm glad you plucked up the courage to be cheeky again, sweetheart. I was thinking of wrapping up quickly, but it looks like you changed my mind."

Someone squeaks. It may have been me.

"Let's see, how many lashes did you just earn... five, I would say. Combined with the twenty I was originally going to give you, that's twenty-five."

I groan. "Great, my favorite number."

"Thirty."

It only takes six lashes to make me cry again, and three after that to make me seriously consider saying my safeword. But I hold my tongue. Hold out for just a few seconds longer—

—and something cracks.

It starts as a buzzing. Subtle at first, but growing stronger. It slides across my skin like caressing hands, gradually expanding to envelope all of my body, bestowing cool, tingling relief everywhere it touches. The sensation creeps up the nape of my neck and reaches my cranium, rushes into my mind in a flood of pure, white light—harsh light, light that scours the inside of my brain and cleanses it of every cluttering thought or emotion. The only thing left is... peace. Surrender. No obligation to do anything but just let go, and feel. Feel the last licks of the whip gracing my back, feel the buzzing slipping down my spine to every last reach of my body, feel the tear tracks cooling on my wet cheeks and a moan gently vibrating in my throat.

Fuck, I missed this. I needed this. Why did I avoid it for so long? I don't remember. I don't... I...

It takes me a few seconds to realize Laylah's stopped hitting me. She loops the whip's braided tail around my neck, letting it graze my exposed throat like the scaled hide of a boa constrictor. She leaves it there as a makeshift collar and steps around me to tower over my limply hanging form. When I look up at her, I see the beautifully stark, severe lines of her face outlined by the light—and in that same light I see the air around me is wreathed in pink, swirling, crackling energy, like my own personal electric field. So much power, so much energy that I'm tempted to draw into myself, to bask in... but I already promised it to her.

Laylah leans down toward me, eyes half-lidded, and breathes the pink energy in through her nose. She exhales it through her mouth like cigarette smoke as she peels off her gloves, one by one.

"*Guten appetit,*" she coos, lighting five fingertips onto the curve of my jaw. And she kisses me.

She tastes like lipstick and pomegranates and it's like she's sapping the air right out of my lungs. I feel the cloud of energy around me surge into her form, feel her take it from me as easily as if she were downing a glass of wine. Every point of contact between her skin and mine—her lips on my lips, her fingertips on my jaw—is a tingling conduit, an open wound. Her other hand reaches around to lie flat on the tight, hot skin of my upper back; I shudder, and I melt.

...She chokes. Icy, scalpel-sharp pain slices across my chest as the severed connection snaps back on me like a rubber band. I sway on the chains, gasping, the room reeling around me. A few more seconds of vertigo give way to a stomach-churning plunge—and then there's nothing but hollow, crestfallen loss.

"*Mistress,*" I whisper, voice cracking. No response. I'm lost and alone, groping in the dark for a familiar shape. *"Mistress?"*

Lifting my head is a Herculean task, but I manage it. My eyes focus on Laylah bent over, clutching her stomach with one hand and covering her mouth with the other as she spasms with a series of violent coughs.

"Laylah?" I call, weakly.

"I'm—I'm fine," she says, coughing a few more times. "Just had—a bit of a shock."

"What happened?" The cavity of my chest aches with emptiness. My breath hitches in my throat. "A-are you finished?"

She straightens up, adjusting her catsuit, clearing stray hairs from her face. "Yes, I think so, my dear." Pink fog drifts in the space between us, making her eyes look like distorted purple gems.

"But... there's still so much left, you're sure you don't want it?"

She purses her lips and rests two fingertips on them, face screwed up in thought. "Your magic is like... caramel. Delicious and sticky and overwhelmingly sweet, but not healthy in large quantities. I only had a taste and I'm already on the verge of nauseous."

"Oh." I made her sick. *My magic* made her sick. I want to crawl into a dark hole and never come out. "I'm so sorry…"

"No need to apologize, it's the best dessert I've had in months. Besides, you fulfilled your end of the bargain perfectly. Let's get you down, and then we'll go see who you came to see."

She unwinds the whip from around my neck—I'd forgotten it was even there—and puts it aside. She unshackles my wrists too, letting them down one by one so I can adjust to the inevitable pins and needles. My emotional stability is shot to Hell, that's for sure. But at least the magical haze is still there. It buoys me up, inside and around me, joining Laylah's hands in supporting my weight as I struggle to stay upright. I wobble over to the bench where I left my clothes, letting my fingers follow the familiar routine of fastening buttons and tying laces without my brain's input. I'm fully dressed, I think. But then I realize I'm standing stock-still, facing a blank wall, with my sports bra in one hand and my necktie in the other. I roll them both up and stuff them into separate coat pockets.

When I'm ready, Laylah takes me back out into the hallway, tugging her gloves back on as she walks. She sticks her head into what appears to be a breakroom.

"Nelly!" she calls.

"Yeah?"

The woman that answers is a smallish blonde in the most clichéd Catholic schoolgirl outfit I've ever seen, down to the skimpy plaid skirt and shirt knotted just under her breasts, revealing a rosy pink abdomen and frilly bra. Damn, I went to Christian school for twelve years and I *never* got to see that. Through a curtain of strawberry blond hair, I can see a lit cigarette sticking out from between her glossy lips.

"Someone wants to talk to you. It's about a client."

"Cop?" Her voice rasps soft and high.

"No, someone else. A friend. *My* friend."

The emphasis seems important somehow; Nelly relaxes her shoulders and stubs her cigarette out in an ashtray. "Come in, come in," she says, like a housewife welcoming dinner guests, dispelling the smoke still hanging in the air with a few waves of her hand.

Laylah makes herself comfortable on a nearby armchair and starts flicking through channels on the TV. I sit down next to Nelly. Her eyes are streaked with so much makeup that she's practically a raccoon.

"Hi, I'm Harry," I say. "Nelly, right?"

"Yup." She leans back in her seat, gauging me with a single sweep of her eyes. Laylah's endorsement seems to have eased her mistrust of me somewhat, but she's still guarded.

"I'm looking for a missing person—Tristan Meresti. He's one of your regulars, right?"

She snorts so loudly I start in my seat. "He used to be. Not anymore, thank *god*."

I frown. "Why, did something happen?"

She nods vigorously. "Listen, I only put up with him because he was good for the money, and because he was easy to please—but holy shit, that got out of hand *fast*. At first he just wanted to fuck me in-session, which isn't that unusual, and he backed off when I said no. Then he asked me out on a date at his place—again, not unheard of, but still super dicey. I let him down easy, and he seemed okay with that. He actually seemed nice up to that point. Maybe a bit lovesick, but still harmless, you know? But then he waited outside the building for *five hours* until I finished my shift and came out. Five... fucking... hours. I nearly had a heart attack when I saw him around the corner."

The hairs on the back of my neck are standing up. "He didn't hurt you, did he?"

She starts to shake her head, but hesitates. "He just... followed me. Kept begging for me to give him a chance, said he was a good guy, said he loved me so much it hurt. And the people walking by, they totally noticed him, but no one took it seriously— this woman was laughing, and some guy fucking *saluted* him. I thought I was losing my fucking mind, it made no sense how I could be so terrified when no one else around me was. Then we got to a stoplight, and he tried to grab me—but someone had their phone out, thank god, and he got distracted trying to get them to stop filming him. I ran as soon as the light changed."

As she speaks, her hands start shaking. They reach to her side, seemingly without her knowledge, extracting a cigarette from a carton and lighting it with mechanical movements.

"Fuck, but that scared me more than it should've. If it was just a bit later at night I would've been walking home in the dark, with less people around. He's scrawny, I had my keys and my pepper spray,

I could have taken him, right? But still..." She sucks on her cigarette like it's an inhaler, then closes her eyes and blows the smoke out in one long, shaky breath. It's probably not a good time to tell her that Tristan's secretly a mage with the ability to shoot fire from his hands. "God, it was so creepy. It's okay though, I haven't seen him since then. He's on security's blacklist, and if I'm scared to walk alone from work I can always call Laylah." She shoots a warm smile in Laylah's direction. Laylah returns it, along with a wink. Nelly turns back to me. "Laylah's a really good bodyguard, she can be *ridiculously* intimidating when she wants to be. I mean, I guess that's a given for a dominatrix. But I've seen her get scary—not like, sexy-scary, I mean really, *really* scary—"

Nelly blinks as though seeing me for the first time. Her cigarette dangles limply from her lips.

"Oh—shit. Crap. I just unloaded so much crap on you, didn't I? I'm so sorry, I just completely...fuck."

I smile reassuringly. "No, it's fine, really. I asked, you answered. Plus it's good to know he's not bothering you anymore."

She screws up her face. "But none of what I just said helps, does it? You said he went missing?"

"Yeah, he did. Actually... you said something earlier, about him asking you out to his place. Did he happen to give you an address?"

Her eyes light up. "Holy shit, I almost forgot!" The cigarette drops from her lips—she catches it and tosses it into the ashtray within seconds. Then she twists around and hefts a heavy, hardcover textbook from the couch behind her. I sneak a peek at the cover before she opens it.

"*Advanced JavaScript: Fourth Edition*," I read out loud. "Are you in school?"

"Mm-hmm. I've wanted to learn programming since I was a kid. Wanted to make video games." She chuckles a little to herself. "What'd you study?"

"I never went to college."

"So what *do* you do?"

"Uh…" I duck my head, awkwardly scratching the back of my neck.

"Oh right, you're one of Laylah's friends. Never mind, I probably don't want to know."

There's a slip of paper, covered in spiderweb creases from being crumpled up at some point, tucked between the textbook's pages as a bookmark. "Here," she says, handing it to me. "He left this behind after a session—probably thought he was being subtle. Probably thinks I'm going to mail myself there in a cake. Asshole. Jeez, look at that handwriting."

"I know, right?" I scan the words quickly. Financial District, 50th floor penthouse suite of a building that's definitely not Meresti property. "Thanks, Nelly," I say, stuffing the paper into my pocket. She flashes a smile around a newly-lit cigarette.

"I'll escort you out," Laylah says, clicking off the TV and rising lithely from the couch.

She leads me back out to the lobby of naked man-butt, then to the door. I take one last look inside the place before stepping across the threshold.

"I might come back here," I muse. Laylah grins, leaning forward out the doorway to match my height.

"Please do," she purrs, slyly giving me a view down her cleavage. "Although, next time I'll have to charge regular rates."

I pout. "What, my delicious diabetic magic isn't good enough for you?"

She tips my chin up with a gloved finger. "It *is* good," she drawls, "But I guarantee, the things I can make you feel when I'm being paid... they'll be worth a *thousand* of your sweetest kisses."

She's barely touched me, but echoes of buzzing pleasure are running up and down my spine again. I shiver, eyes half-closing, knees weak. She chuckles, and I can feel her breath grace my cheek.

"Goodbye, blood witch. I hope you and your politically-inclined employer find what you're looking for."

She keeps me dangling for just a moment longer. There's no strength in my limbs yet I'm locked in place, waiting, waiting, waiting, the finger at my chin a firebrand, her presence right in front of my nose a teasing challenge.

The door shuts. I swallow a disappointed groan and walk away.

CHAPTER 7
DEAR SISTER

I leave the sex dungeon intending to head straight for Tristan's penthouse, but the residual energy from the whipping derails that plan entirely. My skin tingles with it, my head spins with it; it's potent as Hell, but I only have up to an hour before it fizzles away. And letting that happen would be like shooting a gift horse in the foot.

I waltz into my apartment and slam the door with a flourish. My limbs feel loose and weightless — I spin in a circle with my arms out wide, laughing breathlessly. I toss my tie in the vague direction of my desk, do a little skip over to the refrigerator. Let's see, bottles, bottles, do I have any bottles...? Aha! I grab a bottle of soju from the back of the fridge and shake it to watch the liquid sloshing at the bottom. I unscrew the lid and gulp down the last few swallows (should it worry me that I barely feel the burn?), then purse my lips and blow.

Energy bursts from my mouth as a swirling cloud, dark and ominous when filtered through the bottle's translucent green shell. It makes a noise too, a soft, crooning whisper that echoes over and over within the glass confines. I keep blowing until the bottle is brimming, then shut the lid. The excess energy I release into the air as a single, cherry-red puff—it lingers for a moment, then dissipates with the faint, spreading scent of pomegranates. *Nice*.

My knees give out from under me. I stumble, catching the countertop with my free hand. My vision blurs, and I rub the wet corners of my eyes on my sleeve. Am I really that tired? There's a heavy throbbing deep in the muscles of my upper back, and my skin burns where it touches my shirt. Shit, that actually hurts. That hurts a *lot*.

Leaving the bottle at the counter, I lurch to the bathroom. Peeling off my shirt is an ordeal in and of itself, but the real shock comes when I twist around to catch a glimpse of myself in the mirror. *Yikes*. My entire upper back has been swallowed up by a mass of criss-crossing welts and bruises, mostly red and purple but making enthusiastic progress toward black and blue. Poking at a line of raised skin the exact dimensions of the rubber strap Laylah used on me, I go temporarily blind with pain.

Thank the gods there's no blood. I have to hand

it to Laylah, she really knows her stuff. And I'm really bad at remembering where my limits are.

The doorbell chimes. I yank my shirt back on and am still redoing the buttons as I shuffle to the door to check the peephole. At first, I see nothing. Then I point my gaze downward and catch sight of an oversized, floppy black hat. I fumble with the lock and haul open the door.

"Hey Luce!" I say, grinning wide.

Luce peers up at me from under the brim of her hat, a worried crease between her eyebrows. Her ebony skin and sable sundress cut a clear figure against the hallway's flowery wallpaper, and she's clutching the strap of her purse with both hands.

"Are you okay?" she says, "Someone told me you got black-bagged by the Merestis, and when I called you wouldn't pick up your phone."

"Oh, right. Sorry, my phone's kind of… smashed. Here, come on in."

I step aside, and Luce enters the apartment. "What happened?" she asks, taking off her hat and revealing the fluffy purple bob underneath. Her eyes, pools of night sky each dotted with a gleaming star, do a quick sweep around the room and settle back onto me.

"Remember that job you passed to me? The one you got from a 'messenger of a messenger?'"

Luce's eyes widen in alarm. "That was the Merestis?"

"Uh, kind of. It was *a* Meresti. He wasn't really speaking for all of them."

Luce and I sit on the couch while I fill her in on what's going on. I skim over some details, like the number of times I almost died in the sewers, as well as the tiff I had with Miriam. Laylah, I don't mention at all. I just say that I checked on the lead Miriam gave me, and that I have a location sussed out. Luce listens to the whole tale with a thoughtful twist to her violet-painted lips.

Once I'm finished recounting, she says, "So your next step is to find this shithead and drag him back to Miriam, right?"

"Yeah, it's pretty straightforward from here. And don't worry, I know I can take him. I got creamed last time because the Lockharts had his back, but they've thrown him to the wolves now."

The corner of Luce's mouth quirks up. "The 'wolves' being you, Miriam's collared bloodhound?"

"I guess so, yeah." I lick my lips and find my throat parched. "You want a drink?"

Luce nods, and I get up from the couch to go to the fridge. As I open the door, the raw skin over my shoulder blade rubs against my shirt, and I let out a quiet hiss.

I can *feel* Luce stiffen across the room. "Harry?" she says, a high note of alarm in her voice.

"I'm fine!" I call over my shoulder. "Seriously, I'm—"

"*Harry.*"

I stop. Shut the refrigerator door. I turn slowly, dreading the moment Luce sees the guilt etched into my face.

"Luce, I—"

"Take off your shirt." She's standing now, small fists clenched at her sides.

My smile is weak. "What, no foreplay? And I thought *I* was—"

"Take. Off. Your *goddamn* shirt."

I do as she says, quickly unbuttoning my shirt and slipping it off my shoulders.

"See?" I say, spreading my arms wide and showing her my unmarked chest. "I'm perfectly fine."

"Stop patronizing me. I'm the best damn blood witch in the city, and I know when someone's hurt. Turn around."

Luce doesn't even have to raise her voice to scare me. Maybe it's because she's my sister, or because she's had seven years to figure out where all my buttons are. But she has a way of freezing me with sincerity alone, of standing perfectly still and drowning me in the immediate understanding that whatever I've done is just fundamentally *wrong*.

"Okay, okay, just—it wasn't Miriam, okay? It wasn't the Merestis, it was a sex thing, it was consensual. Okay?"

Luce sighs. "Yes, fine, got it. Just show me how bad it is."

I turn around.

Luce sucks in a sharp breath. I bite my lip, fighting off the bubbling guilt.

"Harry, what did you *do*?"

"The lead Miriam gave me was a, um, sex dungeon. There was a succubus domme there with information, and in return for it she wanted to beat the crap out of me. She kind of skimped on aftercare."

"What, you couldn't just fuck her like any other self-preserving witch?"

"Well she was a special case, that wasn't really an option—Luce?"

I turn around to find Luce rubbing her temples with her closed fists, looking like an adorable red panda. A really pissed-off red panda, but still a cute one.

"Harry," she says quietly, clenching her teeth, "You have to have *boundaries*. You can't let every mildly attractive woman within a five-mile radius beat you to a pulp just because you don't *mind*."

"Well it's not just that I don't mind, I do get sexual stimulation out of—"

She purses her lips and glares at me. I try a different tactic.

"It was for the job—"

"Just get on the bed, okay?"

She storms away to rummage through her purse. I trudge to the bedroom and, carefully, flop face-down onto the creaky mattress. I reach for a pillow, then bite back a grunt at the ensuing stab of pain in my shoulder. After another moment of struggling, Luce's hand appears and yanks the pillow in my direction.

"Thanks," I breathe, adjusting the fluffy mass

under my cheek. She doesn't respond. I feel her settle onto the backs of my thighs, and then something cold and runny drips onto my back. "Ah! Fuck!"

"It's just coconut oil, dumbass." She spreads it carefully across my irritated skin while I grit my teeth and tighten my fists into the pillow. "Jesus, what a mess. Not sloppy though. It should be relatively easy to clean up."

"Of course it's not sloppy. It was done by a professional, remember?"

"Hmm."

When Luce makes that noise it means she's finished listening to me. I pout at the wall in retaliation. Then I feel the first of the broken blood vessels knit back together, and my relieved sigh takes even me by surprise.

Luce continues to slide her palms over my back, the oil helping her along. At first the pain subsides just a little, but, as she keeps working, the healed segments of skin and muscle start to blossom with warm, glowing relief. I sink into the mattress, eyelids fluttering. My magic breathes with me, unspooling beyond my physical body as an aimless, living aura.

I'm almost asleep when I feel the tendrils of Luce's magic lapping against my own. It's at once a physical feeling, extending from Luce's palms into the skin of my back, and an abstract one, like one thought intruding on another.

"Luce," I mumble, "If you wanted to feel my

magic you could have just asked."

"Sorry, I didn't want to disturb you."

Luce pokes around a bit. I don't mind. With another witch this kind of interaction might be weirdly intimate, but with Luce it's more like having my hair braided at a sleepover. Not that I've ever experienced that. But, if I had, I assume it would have felt similar.

She approaches the chunk of dead magic centered on the scar at my neck; I stiffen and immediately retract my magic into myself.

"Harry, there's no point in hiding old scars from me. I'm the one who patched them up, remember?"

"Sorry. Reflex reaction."

I unfurl again, and this time when Luce prods, I make an effort not to flinch. The magic in that particular spot is rotten to the core. It's not painful when Luce touches it, just... awkward. Unnecessary. Like poking roadkill. Luce somehow makes the whole process seem clinical, like a doctor examining my mouth with a stale-tasting popsicle stick.

Something occurs to me, and my eyes pop open.

"Hang on, are you checking up on me?"

"Hmm?"

"You are, you're totally checking up on me. Luce, I'm *fine*. The whole succubus thing was just regular sexy masochism. I'm not self-destructing again, I swear."

"I know." Her voice is intentionally blank.

"It was for the job. And for kinky fun. It had

nothing to do with Johanna."

"I never said it did."

I can't think of another response. I just stay quiet as Luce's hands continue to trace patterns over my raw skin, expertly stitching up the internal ruptures. I call up the memory of another time Luce had her hands on me like this—except I was in a lot more pain back then, more pain than I'd ever experienced in my life, and there hadn't been a bed, just a cold, hard, wooden floor. A ritual circle surrounding me, painted onto the floor in stark white. An empty syringe, dropping silently from my hand to roll under the desk. Luce, dragging my twitching, convulsing body into her lap, blue-hot magic sparking from her fingertips to skitter across splintered skin.

I remember her sobbing and begging me not to die. I remember being so scared I almost didn't listen to her.

Almost.

"Done."

I'm a little slow to react to Luce's voice, too wrapped up in memories. "What was that?"

"I'm done. You're good." She pats my back, then slides off the bed.

"Thanks." I prop myself up on my elbows and cautiously sit up. I roll my shoulders, feeling the muscles in my back slide and bunch, then reach back and feel around. Other than a bit of stickiness from the coconut oil, everything is good as new.

"Don't get yourself fucked up again, at least not

until this job's finished. Understood?" Luce calls from the bathroom as she washes her hands.

"Yes ma'am." I roll my neck, groaning at the pins and needles straightening themselves out within the newly-repaired tissue.

"Do you need anything else?"

"Nah, I'm good. Seriously, Luce, thanks." Luce hefts her purse and hat while I put on a new shirt, and I accompany her to the exit. Using my foot to prop open the door, I lean against the doorframe. "By the way, how's it going with Ash? You guys finally went on that date, right?"

She winces. "Yeah, it went... not good. After I told her I was a healer, she spent the rest of dinner ranting about how 'blood magic is a danger to yourself and others,' and that true healing only comes from the 'internal application of rare gemstones.'"

I blink in confusion. "Internal?"

"Vaginal."

My foot slips. The door bangs painfully into my ankle. "Oh. Gods. Tell me she wasn't—not while you were talking—"

"She had a malachite stone up her vagina. While we were talking."

I stare at Luce in horror. She stares back, her face as solemn as an undertaker's.

"But—isn't that toxic or something?"

"Hell if I know. She wouldn't let me check her with magic, so I dropped her off at Planned Parenthood. Hopefully, the nurses there took care of her."

We shudder in unison.

"The whole 'no dating civilians' rule sucks," Luce sighs. "I mean, I get why it's a thing, but trying to be in a relationship with another witch is so—so—" She makes a strangled noise through her teeth as her hands throttle an imaginary neck.

"Why not date another werewolf?" I say, grinning.

She smacks me in the bicep with her purse.

"Ow!"

"You don't get to say shit about my teenage sweethearts, Miss I-Banged-My-Sister's-English-Teacher-For-Three-Months."

Clutching my arm in feigned agony, I open my mouth to speak—Luce cuts me off.

"Besides, I didn't date Ximena because she was a werewolf. She was quiet, but... I liked her a lot. She was sweet." Luce drops her eyes, holding her floppy hat to her chest as her fingers fiddle with the brim. It's hard to tell from my height, but I'd swear she's wearing a bashful smile.

...She puts on the hat, obscuring her face from my view. When she looks up again, she's still smiling, but it's more of a friendly expression.

"Good luck on the case, Harry. I'd come with you to kick this creepy fucker's ass, but I have a high-priority patient to check on, and I don't think Miriam would appreciate another interloper in her family affairs. You can take one apprentice, right?"

"I have to. Otherwise it'd be embarrassing."

She snorts, her smile morphing into a full grin. I grin in return. She says goodbye and turns to leave. I step back into my apartment—

—and catch sight of the darkened soju bottle still sitting on the kitchen counter. I race back out into the hallway, arms flailing.

"Luce! Wait! Can you help me with one more thing?"

CHAPTER 8
IS IT HOT IN HERE, OR IS THAT JUST THE HELLFIRE?

Tristan's penthouse is a bust. The building is there alright, and I have no doubt in my mind that the little weasel's stowed himself away in the top floor suite. Problem is, the top floor is so damn *hard* to reach.

My first plan of entry is ingeniously simple: I stroll into the lobby through the revolving door and make a casually inconspicuous beeline toward the elevators. At least, I *think* it's inconspicuous. I haven't taken six steps across the polished marble floor before the concierge, a primly made-up woman dressed in beige, leans over her desk to say, "Hello, excuse me, are you a registered visitor?"

As it turns out, it's *seriously* difficult to bluff a luxury apartment concierge, especially one who's used to dealing with the impossible whims and fancies of clientele like Tristan Meresti. And it's not as though I can just tell her who I'm here for, much less what I'm planning to do to him. The only thing I gain from the whole exercise is a massive, hand-shaped ache in my shoulder as the burly doorman "assists" me in my exit.

Crap.

I find a payphone a block over and dial the number Miriam gave me. An orchestra furiously plays Beethoven on the other end for about twenty seconds before she picks up.

"Who the *Hell* is this?" There's heavy footsteps in the background, livid shouts. Miriam herself sounds harried and out of breath.

"Hey Miriam, it's Harry. I—"

"Did you get the sword?"

"No, not yet, I think I know where it is but—"

"Then *find* it! It's chaos in this goddamn house right now, Tristan left fucking *bombs* behind!"

My breath stops up in my throat. "Wait—what?"

"This was the Lockharts' play all along, something stopped them from taking the sword from Tristan but it doesn't matter, because they don't need it, because that stupid fucking bootlicker planted *explosive wards* at their request—"

"Holy shit, are you okay?"

"—and we don't know how many there are or whether they're on a timer or where it's safe to move

Matthew, the stress alone could destroy him—"

"Miri! Are you okay?"

"Huh? Yes we're fine, three nurses and an apprentice were burnt but they'll survive. The problem is, we have to sweep the rest of the place while maintaining the perimeter around the city, and our network is already stretching thin—" There's a rustling noise, like the receiver on her side's been muffled by fabric. I can still hear Miriam's voice shouting, "For the last time, Silas, the infirmary is clear! Do as I said and take your team to the Green Hall labs! If we lose Murdoch's spine fluid research it's on *your* head!" The rustling stops, and Miriam's voice comes through clearly again. "If you don't have the sword, you'd better be calling for a good reason, what is it?"

"Uh..." *Hey Miri, could you and your family just send over a mercenary or two, preferably someone who's good at cat burgling?* It didn't seem like such a big request two minutes ago, but now I'm rethinking things. "Never mind. I'll figure it out."

"Oh, for the love of—"

There's a muffled *BOOM* in the background, accompanied by shrill screaming. Miriam shouts something above the din, a command I can't hear—and the line cuts off. I stare at the payphone receiver for a few seconds more, then hang it back up on its hook.

So, I hadn't really had a time limit before, just a wishy-washy "get it done, but you can stop for lunch along the way." And I still have no ominous hourglass or enchanted alarm clock to reference, just the frailty of an old man's life. You could say I'm on a… *dead*line.

The pun loses most of its cleverness when I remember that Miriam and her brother could be dead by tomorrow. Not all of its cleverness, just… most.

I hurry back to the enormous apartment building—around the side, outside of the doorman's field of view—and crane my neck, staring up the glassy, pristine wall. I'll do as I told Miri; I'll figure something out. Hire a mercenary myself, maybe. Or come up with some kind of disguise spell. But first, I need to know what tools I have available. And to do that, I need to go back home.

***

I take a cab back to my place. Ride the elevator up to the fourth floor, fumble with my keys for a good half-minute. Open the door, enter, shut the door. Turn on the lights and turn around.

"Hi," says the demon standing in my apartment.

I pause for a few seconds, doing all my startled screaming internally so as to save face. With my outward expression kept carefully neutral, I respond with a simple, "Hi."

She grins, and a tail peeks out from behind her legs to lash from side to side. It's a lion's tail, long and flexible and topped with a tuft of fur that matches her hair. I twist back to look at the doorframe; the lock isn't broken, and my discreetly carved warding sigils are untouched. I turn slowly back toward her.

"How did you get in?"

"The window." She tosses her head backward, making her thick black hair bounce. I walk past her to the open window and run my hand along the sill. Like the ones at the door, all the warding sigils are strangely intact.

"You're the one who's been following me the last few days, right?" I say, sliding the window shut.

"Mm-hmm," her voice rumbles from right behind me. This time I do startle, and when I whirl around I'm met with eyes of molten gold. She regards me with her chin tipped upward, her wide grin tamed into an easy smile. She leans into me; I breathe in, and forget to breathe out.

"...What's your name?" I manage.

Her eyes flicker up to the ceiling. She pushes her plump bottom lip out to one side. Then she says, with a certain decisiveness, "Lilith."

That's a fake name if I've ever heard one. I already know she can't hurt me, but it's still comforting to know she's being cautious in my presence, just as I am in hers.

"Okay, Lilith," I say, sidling out from between her and the window, making my way to the desk. With the window closed and all the sounds of the street banished, my voice echoes loud and clear. "Did someone hire you to follow me?"

"If you're talking about that kid with the greased hair, no."

"Then why—"

"Because I was curious." She hops onto my desk in one fluid movement, dropping into an easy crouch. She sweeps her eyes up and down my form. Flicks her tail once. "I heard some neighbors complaining about a witch who survived demon blood. I wanted to know what she was like."

I'm distracted by the fangs bared in my direction, just for a second. Then I realize what she's said. "That's old news. Fourteen months old. Where have you been?"

She shrugs. "Out of the loop, I guess. Like you."

Her bare shoulders are a rich, coppery brown that contrasts with the lightness of her clothing. I don't think I've ever met a demon who wears white. There are two open slits in the side seams of her dress around the level of her ribs, the purpose of which I can't tell. I guess she likes her clothes airy?

"Were you dead?"

"Nope."

"Then how did you do that?" I drape my coat over the back of my chair and sit down. I lean back so I can look up at her. "Stay out of the loop—as a demon, I mean. I thought gossip spreads fairly quickly in Hell."

"Not to me." She kicks out her legs to sit on the edge of the desk, imitating my posture, her bare feet dangling down to brush my knees. Ooh, lion feet. With claws. Better be careful of those. "I'm kind of in the others' blind spot. They don't much care for me, and I'm mostly on Earth anyway."

That's weird. I've talked to demons with established lives on Earth. They usually adapt more to human society, sticking mostly to human form, getting jobs, even paying taxes. Lilith doesn't seem to be making an effort to fit in.

"How did you get in?" I ask again.

Again, she responds with, "The window."

"I know that. How did you get past the wards?"

She cocks her head and smirks. Doesn't answer. I furrow my brow in frustration—until a thought occurs to me.

"Hold on, did you climb up here?"

"Mm-hmm."

"All four stories?"

"Yep." She pops the 'P' like a cherry.

"Hypothetically, if there were a penthouse with glass windows about, say, fifty stories high, could you carry someone up there?"

"You mean the greasy kid's treehouse?"

Oh, right. I'd forgotten about the whole stalking thing. "Yeah, that place. Could you get me in?"

She snorts. "Is that even a question? I break into places like that for fun." One side of her lips quirks up, baring the slightest hint of ivory. "Why? Does the big bad blood witch need some help?"

"I do, actually." I lean forward, and she meets me halfway so that our faces are inches apart. "What's it going to cost me?"

She pushes out her lip again, hums as though deep in thought. She startles me by springing off the desk to meander across the office, humming even more loudly, arms held innocently behind her back. I watch her closely; she's walking nimbly on her toes, like a ballerina en pointe, but with none of the effort. She stops in front of my bookshelf and flicks a random title with her finger. Then she pirouettes to face me again, her grin splitting her face from ear to ear.

"Your soul."

Godsdammit. I slump back in my chair, frowning. "Look, if you don't want to help me you might as well just say—"

"*I'm not fiiiiinished.*"

Her sing-song voice sets off all my alarm bells. Still, I stay quiet and hear her out. She makes her way back to me, just as slowly as she left.

"I'm not going to help you damn yourself; you can do that on your own time. But the second you show up in Hell all sad and mopey, your soul belongs to me, and only me. *If* you get damned."

I chew it over in my head. "So... it's not really a deal so much as a bet."

Her grin splits so wide that the whole rest of her *glitches*—I catch the barest glimpse of an alternate form. Big, *big* alternate form. It's over in a millisecond though, and then she goes right back to being a gorgeous woman with a glittering smile and a belly that'd be heaven to rest my head on.

I take a deep breath. "Okay, so if I take this deal, you'll help me with Tristan whether or not I'm damned. But if I fuck up later down the road and end up in Hell, you get to keep my soul in a jar or...

eat it, or whatever the Hell demons do with souls down there. Do I have that right?"

She gives a single, slow nod.

"But if I don't fuck up, and I don't get damned before I die... then nothing happens. My soul fucks off to Purgatory while you sit around and stew."

She nods again.

I furrow my brow. "So wait, how is this a good investment for you? Are you really that sure I'm going to get damned?"

She shrugs with one shoulder. "Who knows what you'll get up to before you die? You did try to resurrect your dead mentor with demon blood."

Every muscle in my body locks up.

"I didn't try to resurrect her."

She snorts. "Sure you didn't. Even Hell knows your sister was covering for you in court. Imagine how much bigger the fuss would have been if they'd been able to prove you were attempting necromancy—two forbidden birds, one stone, phew. I would've loved to be a fly on that wall—"

SLAM.

"I didn't try to resurrect her."

I'm standing with my palms flat against the surface of my desk, taking in air in ragged gasps. When did I get up? There's a belated *thump* as my chair, which has been steadily rolling away, hits the wall.

Lilith blinks at me from where she's standing. I'm breathing hard, but she's still as a ceramic vase.

"...Sure," she says, looking at me a little oddly.

"Whatever you say."

I swallow. "Sorry, I—it's a touchy subject." My scar throbs. I rub at it angrily with the heel of my hand, turning toward the wall. I drop my head and inhale deeply, closing my eyes—and flash on an image of torn and bloodied silk, damply clinging to ruptured flesh.

No. Don't think about that. Don't *picture* that. Are you really going to cry in front of a *demon*? Just breathe. I collect the scattered pieces of myself, one at a time, as well as my thoughts.

The lives of Miriam and her whole family ride on this. For fuck's sake, there are *children* in that family. I can take this deal, right now, and get going with smashing both elbows into Tristan's prettyboy nose. But even if I weren't exactly selling my soul, I'd be... bonding myself... to Lilith. To a demon. And the last time I did that, I—I wasn't ready, I didn't think—I—*he*—

But every second I delay, Matthew Meresti crawls his decrepit skeleton closer and closer to the void. I could chase Lilith off and try to find an alternate path, but that's going to take time no matter what. And none of the Merestis have time to spare.

Take the deal, risk screwing myself over. Don't take the deal, risk screwing Miriam over... again.

That's not even a decision, is it?

"...okay," I say, my voice getting stronger as I speak. "Okay." I turn around and step carefully out from behind the desk, leaving no barrier between

Lilith and me. I straighten out my tie and collar, looking her square in the eye. "I'm taking the contract. How do we seal it?"

The briefest silence, a widening of her eyes. Then her grin cleaves her face like a knife wound. Her pupils narrow into cat-like slits a second before she lunges at me.

My back hits the wall with a *THUMP*. I let out a startled grunt, sparks at the edge of my sight. Shadows fall as she looms over me, growing to—six feet? Seven feet? I watch with hazy vision as her sclera fill with black and her teeth lengthen into jagged points, horns like ridged coal shards bursting through her temples. She rips off my tie and tears open my shirt, then pins my shoulders to the wall with both arms. The sound of grinding, shrieking bone, and a second set of arms erupts from her sides. Oh, so *that's* what the dress slits are for.

She taps a razor-sharp claw against my rib, just below my left breast. Cocks her head to one side. "*May I?*" she says in a dual-toned harmony, her voice splintered into an enthralling soprano and throaty tenor that crackles like an old record. I pause to think of all the different ways Luce is going to upbraid me for this.

"Sure, go ahead."

I suck in a sharp breath through my teeth as she breaks my skin. I almost jerk, but she catches my hip in a bruising grip with her last free arm, anchoring me at three points. Her claw catches as she carves a tightly curled spiral; my legs shake, and a cold sweat breaks out across my forehead.

The path she carves into me wanders first from left to right, then down the length of my torso in a straight line. She moves slowly, methodically, focused entirely on getting the design right regardless of the way I dig my nails into the wall and try to suppress the strangled noises tearing at the inside of my throat. *"Halfway done,"* she mutters in her alien, rumbling voice, almost to herself, as she opens a bloody circle around my bellybutton.

The stinging against my stomach rushes up my spine to the back of my eyes, and the tears finally spill over. I make a noise somewhere between a whimper and a hiccup. Lilith glances up—I forget to breathe, too busy staring at the way her pupils have dilated to nearly eclipse the amber glow of her irises. She looks back down at her work, thick eyebrows knotting in concentration and the ivory points of her canines peeking out from under her pillowy lips. Gods, she's gorgeous. It's not fair, why is evil always so attractive?

Then the pain is back, cutting through my pleasant thoughts like a shark through a school of fish. I jerk and stutter out a swear under my breath.

Her hands tighten on my shoulders and hip in warning.

"Don't. Move."

The finishing touches go on my lower stomach— and then she's done. I barely have a moment to catch my breath before she places her palm flat against the bloody design and grates something in Hellish syllables I can't understand. From between her fingers, my open wounds glow with blinding white light. She presses her forehead against mine, making sure I'm staring straight into her eyes.

"Do you accept the terms of the contract?" she says in English.

"I do," I grit out.

Parted skin rejoins, sutured together by neat lines of scabbing. I lean my head back against the wall, eyes sliding shut, breathing out excess air I hadn't even realized I was holding. When I crack my eyes open again, I find Lilith shrunken back to her original 5'5" form. The only remnants of her demon biology are her tail, feet, and ever-present grin.

"There," she says in a voice brimming with satisfaction, affectionately patting my chest. "We're practically married now."

I'm too exhausted to move from my position against the wall, but I do manage a skeptical eyebrow raise. "Really? I don't know what you think marriage is, but—"

She grabs me by the back of my neck and yanks me down onto her mouth.

The plumpness of her lips cushions my fall. For a moment, shock crowds out sensation—then I'm hit with the scent of flowers. No defined type, just fresh and alive and light enough to be fragile. Her tongue—tongues?—snake out to flicker against my top lip. Oh, it's forked. *Nice*. The knowledge inspires me to slide my hands around her soft, full waist and get just a bit wetter and sloppier in the way I'm kissing her.

She tightens her grip on the back of my neck and forces my lips open with her own—I'm loath to stop sucking on her wonderfully thick lower lip, but I'm also nothing if not accommodating. I try running my tongue up between the fork in hers, and she purrs, honest-to-gods purrs deep in her chest like a cat. I'm just leaning forward when she breaks away from my lips to nuzzle against my cheek, leaving me panting.

The heavy curves of her body are warm against my bare chest. Her breath tickles my ear. "Meet you at the penthouse," she whispers.

And then she's a blurred path to the window, vanishing as quickly as she appeared.

Well. That was fun. I stumble to my desk and collapse into the chair, feeling strangely cold. My stomach is a bloody mess, staining the waistband of my slacks. I'll clean that up. Soon. But for now I just... Wow. I need a moment. I tip my head over the back of my chair and take a deep, shuddering breath before closing my eyes.

***

"What is the first rule of demon deals?"

"Never sell your soul."

Johanna gives a single, firm nod, satisfied with my answer. I huff and lean back in my airy wicker chair.

"Why are you even quizzing me on this? You know I'm not stupid."

Johanna arches an eyebrow. She sips her tea slowly, deliberately, making me wait. "Do I know that? I remember giving you specific instructions not to impede our stay in the vampire king's domain with another one of your impulsive pursuits. And what did you do?"

"It's not like I was drooling after her like some kind of lecher, she's the one who snuck into the guest room —"

"You slept with the vampire princess. In the vampire king's home. You're lucky Lucille had curried enough favor with the queen to delay the execution."

I groan, tipping my head back and letting my arms dangle at my sides, rolling my eyes at the cheery rays of sunshine filtering through the open windows of the living room. The dust motes illuminated against the ceiling are especially pretty today; I scowl at them even harder.

"Fine, I fucked up," I say, voice straining through my extended windpipe. "But come on, what did you expect? They weren't even actual royalty, their 'domain' was a ranch *in Wyoming."*

"Harrietta," Johanna chastises, without a hint of sarcasm in her voice, "We were guests in their home. Therefore, it was our duty to respect the rules and customs of the place, regardless of our personal opinions on their legitimacy. And they had an army of wheat-farmers with pitchforks."

"Okay, okay, I'm sorry, I wasn't thinking straight. But that doesn't give you the right to start treating me like a novice apprentice again. Pop quizzes over tea? Really?" My own milk tea sits untouched in front of me. I'm sure it's delicious, but right now my pride takes priority.

Johanna puts her cup delicately down on her saucer, face betraying no emotion. "If you're really so upset about my treating you like a child, perhaps you should go retrieve your book on manual organic matter reconstruction so we can review a topic more suited to your level. How does that sound?"

I blanch. I hate heavy books and I hate manual healing—Johanna knows that better than I do. I stare her down, hoping to find some sign in her steely gray eyes that she's only joking.

Her irises reflect the streaming sunlight like mirrors. I get nothing from them.

I reluctantly push my chair out from under the little round tea table and trudge toward the foyer.

"Harrietta?" Johanna calls. I stop. Turn around. She's getting up from her seat, robe cascading around her legs like a waterfall. "You know I don't mean to patronize you," she says, stepping forward. "You've grown so much from the child you used to be, and I am so proud of you for it." Something nice and warm flutters in my stomach. She reaches me, lightly touching a hand to my shoulder. "But that worries me too, because there is such a thing as growing up too quickly. You're only twenty-two, Harrietta. You have so much ahead of you, so much left to learn. Things can only become more dangerous from here.

"What I am trying to teach you is that you should never, ever forget the basics. Never forget what you cannot risk. Never forget how easy it is to slip and let all that power get to your head. Because you **are** *a powerful witch, Harrietta. There is no mistaking that."*

I know she can clearly see the pink in my cheeks, but I avoid her gaze and attempt a modest shrug anyway. "Eh, I don't know. I think Luce can outdo me pretty easily now."

Johanna shakes her head. "This isn't about Lucille, Harry, it's about you. I don't worry about her as much because she has had to fight for every scrap of ability she has—it is impossible for her not to understand its value, because she paid such a steep price for it. She will be cautious and diligent, and she will do anything she can to protect what is hers. But I worry that you won't do the same."

I lower my eyes. I wish what she was saying didn't make so much sense. She cups my cheek with a warm palm, making me look up again.

"I only want you to be careful, Harry. You are my first apprentice. I cannot *lose you. Do you understand?"*

Her eyes bore into mine. I swallow, and nod.

"Yes," I say, my voice weak and wavering. I clear my throat and stand up straighter. "Yes, I understand."

"Good." She folds me into her arms and presses a quick kiss to my forehead. My eyelids flutter shut and the tension in my shoulders melts away. She's so warm, always so warm, and she smells like home. But she pulls away after only a moment. "Now go get your book, and I'll reheat your tea."

I nod and turn away, hurrying back to the foyer. At the last second, I glance back.

Johanna smiles at me, crinkling the corners of her eyes and mouth. For a second, she looks older and softer than I've ever seen her. But then the impression is gone, and I find myself padding up the stairs to my room.

It takes a while to sort through the haphazard piles of books and papers cluttering my room. I toss heavy volumes aside with wild abandon, but take the time to stack comic books and zines into organized piles. Where the Hell is my manual healing book? Then I remember — I left it in Luce's room yesterday, when I went to show her a funny diagram. I mince my way across the room, careful not to trip over mounds of dirty clothes, and head over to Luce's.

*The door is locked, adorned with a sign scribbled on pastel pink notebook paper that says, "*DO NOT OPEN!! Experimentation in progress!!!*" What is Luce experimenting with again? Right, she's trying to figure out a way to dye her petticoats with sky projections. She won't kill me if I mess with her petticoats — she'll just make me* wish *I were dead.*

Oh well, guess that means I won't be studying organic reconstruction today. What a pity.

I practically skip back down the stairs, barely suppressing a smile. "Johanna?" I call. "I can't get my book, it's in Luce's room. Is there anything else we —"

Three steps before the bottom of the stairs, I stop. Twisting over the banister to look behind me, I can only see a sliver of the living room through the doorway connecting it to the foyer. Through that sliver I see the whipping of sheer curtains across an open window.

But I can't hear it.

I listen, straining for the sound of fabric flapping against the wind. It has to be there, I can see it happening. But the only thing I can hear is my own breathing. And when I hold my breath, I hear…quiet. Not regular quiet, a kind of quiet that's so absolute it tickles every warning instinct in the back of my lizard brain. No creaking of wooden chairs, no teacups rattling on saucers, no slippers gently padding across the hardwood floor.

Nothing.

A yawning emptiness opens up inside my chest, threatening to swallow me whole. I tear down the rest of the stairs and across the foyer. "Johanna?" *I shout,* "Johanna!"

As soon as I cross the threshold into the living room, sound returns to the world. It rushes into my ears, desperate to be heard—a klaxon of snapping curtains, the remains of a porcelain teapot crunching under my booted feet, two light fixtures fizzing and crackling as they dangle from frayed wires above. Sound barrier. Someone's put a spell around the room to insulate it from the rest of the house, making whatever happened here impossible to hear. Impossible to notice. Impossible to interfere with.

"Joha—"

I slip on something slick and fall forward onto my chin with a sickening CRACK. *My tongue erupts in pain where I've sliced through it with my teeth; I raise my hand to my jaw, gasping. Something sticky smears onto my face.*

Blood. All over my palm. The metallic stench of it, unnoticed before, fills my nostrils and clogs my throat. I trace the trail of oozing red along the floor with my eyes, past a sparse forest of table and chair legs, to a shadowed, crumpled mass.

A moment of numb, ice-cold denial. And then I'm screaming myself hoarse, scrambling forward on my hands and knees, a terrified animal rushing toward danger instead of away.

When Luce comes home, she finds me still kneeling over the body, desperately trying to fix a face that's not there.

CHAPTER 9
THE WORST LAID PLANS OF DEMONS AND LESBIANS

I take a cab to Tristan's penthouse, wearing a clean shirt and pants, absentmindedly reaching between my shirt buttons to finger the raised scab that will undoubtedly become a permanent scar. Demons don't usually leave such prominent marks on their prey. Too much of a hassle, and most civilians balk at the idea of a business contract hinged on scarification. But Lilith is not a normal demon, that much I know for sure. How the Hell did she get past my wards, anyway?

I get out of the cab, pay the driver, and skip around to the side of the apartment building before the testy doorman can recognize me. Once I'm safely out of his line of sight, I take a moment to stare up the side of the building, just as I did the last time I was here. Can Lilith really climb that? There's a number of concrete ledges spaced evenly apart, but the majority of the building's side surface is clear, polished glass. Maybe she can fly?

"I'm ready if you are," Lilith chirps, leaning over my shoulder on her tiptoes. I turn slightly and her face is right next to mine, her warm body pressing against my back.

"Of course I'm ready. I showed up, didn't I?"

"Alrighty then, turn around."

I pivot to face Lilith. She's rocking back on her heels with her arms behind her back, her smile surprisingly non-threatening. But the corners of her mouth are twitching, and by the deepening dimples in her cheeks, I can tell she's making a huge effort not to burst into her usual inhuman grin. I wait for her to do something. She hides a snicker behind a cough. I clear my throat.

"Okay, so how are we—"

I squeak like a chew toy as Lilith clamps her arms around my waist—holy shit, it's like being encircled by iron rails. The sound of her skeleton creaking into a different form happens all at once, and she's suddenly towering above me, hoisting me up and over her shoulder like a towel. Then she leaps into the air, flailing cargo and all.

It's an automatic response to throw my arms around her back and hang on tight. Her hair whips into my face as she bounds up the side of the building, using one set of hands to find even the most invisible ledges to grab as the other keeps me in place. Sometimes, there aren't any handholds at all; in those cases, she simply digs her fingers into solid concrete and makes herself a new one.

Bent over her shoulder as I am, I have a fantastic view of the sidewalk growing further and further away, like I'm zooming out on a satellite map. It's not until I see a rooftop that it finally strikes me how high up I am. A wave of panic crashes down on me, filling up the cavity of my chest with slippery dread and flipping the contents of my stomach upside down. But, just before I vomit a hundred feet down the side of a skyscraper and onto her white dress, Lilith adjusts her grip on my body, wrapping me around her neck like a scarf and securing me by an arm and leg. The panic doesn't disappear, but it subsides just enough for me to watch the city shrink below me with just a bit of awe mixed with the abject terror.

My ears are blocked from the sudden change in altitude, yet I still manage to hear the muffled *CRASH* of Lilith launching both of us through the floor-to-ceiling window of the uppermost apartment. I curl up as best I can, desperate to avoid the shards of glass raining down like hail. The impact of Lilith's feet hitting the floor knocks the breath out of me, and the subsequent momentum snaps my head forward, pushing my face right into her bicep. She carries me away from the glass-strewn portion of the floor and sets me down on a patch of carpet where I can sit, stunned, with a trickle of blood escaping my left nostril.

"Oops," she says, peering curiously down at me as she shrinks back to human form. "You alright?"

"Uh." I don't think I have any strength left in my legs, so I leave them splayed in front of me. "Sure. Yeah." I swallow, and my ears *POP* painfully.

Lilith lights up with a grin. "Good, good. I'll see you around, yeah?" She starts for the her-shaped hole in the window.

"Woah, wait—" I try to get up, but collapse back onto my ass. "You're not going to help me look for the sword? Or at least deal with Tristan?"

She tilts her head. "Why would I do that? It wasn't part of the contract."

"Oh. Right."

She laughs. "You're funny, Witchy. You're smart in a few interesting ways, but pretty dumb in all the others. It's cute."

I blink. "Thanks…?"

"You're welcome. Catch you later!"

Before I can ask when "later" is, she hops deftly out the window, her streaming hair being the last thing to escape my line of sight. I stare at the empty night sky for just a little longer, then check out my surroundings.

There's a massive, shoddily-made bed right next to me, sheets black and white like a domino. Everything in the room is cleanly monochrome—at least, it would be, if there weren't bits of unpainted wood peeking through gouges in the black bedside tables and drawers. And the bed isn't just badly made, the sheets are ruined by uneven gashes and enormous singe marks that still smell faintly of scorched silk. Shards of white porcelain are mixed with the shattered glass on the floor. Tristan's been throwing a tantrum.

Wait, hold on. I fumble with my coat, frantically rooting inside to grab at an object in the deepest, most thickly insulated pocket, wrapped around and around in as many layers of bubble wrap as I could find. When I take it out and unwind the soft plastic, the clear green of my soju bottle peeks through. I check the bottle all around for cracks and thankfully find none—although, if it *had* broken, I'd be suffering the consequences already. Thank the gods for bubble wrap. I stuff the wrapping into an outer pocket and return the bottle to the inside of my coat, where it sits snugly against my ribs.

I hear the thumping of footsteps and twist around just in time for the bedroom door to bang open, revealing Tristan's gaunt figure. Something glitters in his hand—the sword, dangling from his clenched fist by means of a thin chain. Something glints in his other hand too.

Oh *Hell* no.

"Don't fucking move!" Tristan bellows, pointing the handgun straight at my head. I immediately disobey the order and put my hands up in the air as far as they'll go. "*I said don't move!*"

I must be a hot mess, sitting sprawled in the middle of a destroyed room with a bloody nose and a scared-shitless expression. Yet, somehow, Tristan manages to outdo me. His previously immaculate shirt and trousers are more wrinkle than fabric. If he was thin before, now he's a skeleton; his cheekbones look like they're about to burst through his near-translucent skin. His hair doesn't look styled anymore, just plain greasy, hanging over his face like the most unappetizing noodles.

My stomach growls.

"Shut up!" Tristan screams.

"I didn't say anything!"

"Shut up!"

He shakes the gun at me, and I wisely revise my decision to protest again.

"Miriam sent you, didn't she?" he demands, eyes wheeling around the room. The chain is wound so tightly around his fingers that I expect them to turn blue any moment. "Where's the rest of her people? How many are there?"

"It's just me."

"Bullshit!" The sword swings in a wide arc with the force of his exclamation. Tristan glances nervously down at it, then tightens his grip on the chain.

I shake my head. "Nope. No Merestis. No reinforcements."

"Lie to me again and I'll—"

That's my cue to *actually* start lying.

"You absolute bumblefuck, you don't think Miriam wants me dead as much as you? I'm the one who stole the damn sword in the first place—and whose fault is that, huh? I came for the sword, for *leverage* to keep myself *alive*. Get the picture?"

Tristan opens his mouth. Closes it again. Clenches his jaw.

"How did you find the sword?"

"What?"

He thrusts the offending ornament of gold and silver toward me. "The first time, how did you find it?"

"I—" Wait. Slow down. Just for once, don't say the first thing that pops into your head. *Think.* "...You mean, how did I make a finding spell that got through the concealing wards?"

"Of course that's what I mean, you stupid bitch!"

This new information changes the game considerably. Miriam assumed that I was able to locate and enter the gator mole tunnels because of Tristan's sabotage. But if that's not the case, that means I really did get past those wards on my own. Therefore...

"You want my help to get past the barricade around the city, don't you?"

The gun rattles in Tristan's hand. I ramble on.

"You had *no idea* I had a way to get past the Merestis' wards when you hired me."

"Of course I didn't know! You're a crippled has-been who digs up cheap love spells for a living, you were never supposed to find the sword until I *let* you!"

A missing piece, one that neither Miriam nor I had even realized was absent. One that can help fill in some other narrative gaps.

"...And because I found it way ahead of schedule, the Merestis went into full alert before your Lockhart backers could organize your ride out of the city. So they met you in that back alley just to tell you they were abandoning you."

"Stop stalling and get to the fucking point! Tell me how you got past the wards!"

I can't help but crack a lopsided grin at his impatience. "You'd like to know, wouldn't you?"

A bullet hits the floor between my legs with a deafening *CRACK*! I scramble to my feet.

"Okay okay, I have a spell! There's a ritual that goes with it, but I'm the only one Johanna taught it to, you need me alive!"

Tristan doesn't lower the gun, but he does relax his grip on it. The show of power seems to have placated him somewhat, the way milk soothes a crying baby. Ew.

"Where is it?"

"Here, right here." Tristan tenses again as I reach into my coat, but I move slowly enough not to aggravate him further. "It's a bottle. Just a bottle, see? Shoot me and I'll drop it, then we'll both be out of luck."

His eyes remain trained on the bottle as I pull it out of my coat, then widen as he catches sight of the dark cloud roiling within. "Give me that," he demands, striding forward and reaching out, gun carelessly lowered to his side.

I chuck the bottle at his face.

It hits him in the chest—not an unfavorable outcome—and shatters on impact, releasing a mushroom cloud of crimson magic with Tristan at ground zero. As he staggers back in confusion, the magic reels around his face, finds his eyes, and forces its way into the sockets.

Tristan screams. He flails wildly with the gun still in his hand—for a moment I'm terrified that he'll send the sword sailing across the room and out the shattered window. But the chain stays faithfully tangled around his fingers, and as he blindly swings the gun in my direction, I find I have more pressing concerns.

CRACK!

I throw myself sideways just in time to hear the bullet shatter an undamaged piece of window behind me. Glass and ceramic shards slice into my shins and forearms as I scramble for the bed and worm my way under it. The space is too cramped for my gangly limbs, but I'll take any protection I can right now.

It occurs to me, as I watch Tristan's expensive dress shoes stumble across the floor, that I could have just handed the bottle over and convinced him to open it himself. He'd have had to put down the gun, at the very least—but no, I just *had* to be dramatic. I curse and slap my palm against my face.

Another bullet *CRACK*s into the bed frame, splintering wood and making me jump so that my spine scrapes the springy wire net above me. Two more gunshots; I do my best impression of a pillbug, drawing my arms and legs underneath myself, covering my head and praying that the gun's running out of bullets.

One more shot… and then the pronounced *thump* of a body hitting the floor. I look up just in time to see Tristan's handgun clattering onto the bare floor near the wall. A half-beat later, the sword, its silver chain shining like the tail of a meteor, drops silently onto the carpet just two feet from my face.

I snake my arm out from under the bed to snatch it up. The chain is warm to the touch, probably from Tristan's body heat, but the sword is nice and cool. My arms and legs tremble from leftover adrenaline as I crawl out from under the bed. Pushing a few loose strands of hair back from my face, I can see that the sword is unscathed. Thank the gods. I pull the chain around my neck and tuck the sword into my shirt collar.

A miserable, drawn-out wail brings my attention back to Tristan. He's scrabbling at the floor like a rat caught in a mousetrap, alternately reaching out with shaking, claw-like hands and trying to curl up into the smallest ball possible. Every time he flails, howling his distress, shards of glass and porcelain open scarlet gashes in his papery skin. He doesn't notice. The illusion of agony lancing through his mind right now is strong enough to overpower anything in the physical world.

Pleasure and pain, two sides of a very thin coin. Take a bottle of energy skimmed from a masochistic whipping, do some fiddling, and you can convert it into a pretty convenient pain Molotov. It's the same principle that allows one to trap the volatile emotions from a baseball game into a jam jar and transform the whole setup into a makeshift concussion grenade.

Magic. What *can't* it do?

Tristan continues to shriek, completely oblivious to my presence. I consider letting him stew for just a little longer, as payment for the grief he's caused to Miriam, Nelly, me, and no doubt countless others. But then he starts scratching his eyes out.

"Okay buddy, time for bed," I say, hastily dropping to one knee in front of him. I force his hands away from his face where they've already left deep, oozing gouges on his cheeks and throat. He flails for me with bloodied fingernails, blubbering, and I can't tell if he's trying to kill me or begging for my help. I get a good grip on his skeletal shoulders, roll him over, and touch one hand to a bloodstain on the carpet and the other to the back of his neck. I use the spilled blood to draw my magic out and coax it under his skin. Some cautious poking and snaking between muscle fibers—ah, there's the delicate nerve at the top of his spinal column. I trigger the surrounding muscles to give it a firm pinch.

The sobbing and writhing stop. Tristan's limbs, suddenly drained of all their frenzied energy, drop to the floor like rubber hoses. I lean in close to listen to his breathing. It's even, albeit exhausted.

So that takes care of that. I pick the gun up off the floor where it landed earlier and pop the clip out.

Never hurts to be safe, you know? I find a landline phone on the bedside table, feel the satisfying *click click click* of keys under my fingertips as I dial Miriam's number. Beethoven plays again, except this time it somehow sounds more soothing than furious. I kick back and flop onto the ruined bed as I listen, letting my tired muscles sink into the wonderfully soft mattress. I'm almost disappointed when the ringtone cuts off.

"...Harry? Is that you?" There's a worn edge to Miriam's voice. She sounds much quieter than she did the last time I spoke to her.

"Yeah, it's me. Are you guys okay?"

"We're still sweeping the mansion, but Matthew's safe. The gator moles dug out an entirely new bunker some forty feet below our deepest sub-basement to keep him in. The pressure and the unfiltered air are playing havoc with his lungs, but if we really need to we can keep him there for another—"

"It's okay, Miriam. I got the sword."

"—day, and in the meantime I can sneak myself out to—" She stops, finally having processed what I said. "Wait. Did you just say—?"

"I have the sword. Tristan's dealt with too. I just need your people to pick us both up before the cops get here, is that possible?"

There's a second of silence on the other end. Then—

"Oh, thank the Goddess, thank the fucking Goddess—just stay right there, okay? We'll come to you, just—just stay exactly where you are—"

"Will do."

The line clicks shut. I put the receiver back in place and lie limp on the torn-up bed, staring up at the ceiling.

A cold, sharp wind whips into the apartment from the window. It washes over my face, coaxing my eyelids shut. I'm sure the Merestis will be here within the minute; their response time is leagues better than the NYPD's. But that thought doesn't stop me from drifting off, sleep soothing the adrenaline-worn ache in my bones and the stinging of shallow cuts on my skin.

***

The wind is wet and chilly at Johanna's funeral. The sky overhead is a clear, endless blue, but the sun's blanched rays offer no warmth to the faces they touch. No one is required to speak or to listen. The entire event is just an invitation to walk by a closed casket, acknowledge the now non-existence of someone you knew in passing, and move on.

It's not really for Johanna at all. It's more for Luce and me, the two bereaved apprentices struggling to realize we're not apprentices anymore. Luce is bearing that struggle better than I am. She has her head held high, black dress neatly pressed, pink dye wrung out of her hair and replaced with a fishnet veil that leaves her face unobscured while politely telling people to fuck off.

Me? I barely managed to get out of bed this morning. My suit is just as well-tailored as Luce's dress, but at best it's an abandoned window display for a Christmas shop in June. Somewhere deep, deep inside, the real me is hiding under covers and smothering herself with sleep, in a room inside of a room inside of a room. Knock knock, who's there? Knock knock, who's there? Knock knock, knock knock, knock knock...

People bow almost imperceptibly to the casket before they slip away, just as they slipped in and out of Johanna's life — as allies, colleagues, sometimes even friends. But the friends are few and far between. I watch a particular clump of black-clad mages step forward and dip their heads toward the casket in synchronized unison. Then the clump drifts toward Luce and me.

"Harry."

One of the mages is in front of me, peering at me with concerned eyes. Mahogany eyes. I blink, suddenly so tired I could collapse onto the grass right then and there.

Instead, I force my mouth to move. "Miri. Hi."

"How are you doing?"

"Better." *That's a lie. I'm probably in worse shape than I was before, back when Miri first came to check up on me, to hold me tight enough to bruise and let me stain her expensive clothes with snot and tears. But now I'm empty enough that I can at least fake a smile — I do that now, then regret it as Miri balks at the ghastly expression.*

She looks at me, really sees me. "You don't look so good, Harry. You want to go over by the trees for a bit?"

Trees, no people. Just Miri and me. I suddenly realize how much that thought lightens the weight on my shoulders, and nod. Miri glances back toward her family. They seem reluctant — but then one of the older Merestis eeps *as a static shock zaps her in the side. She mouths a quick, distracted "go ahead" to Miriam, snagging the troublemaker by a shoulder. I recognize its owner immediately by the tawny, overgrown bangs tumbling over his eyes; Pax twists around and winks at me as he's pushed away like a shopping cart with a squeaky wheel. Miriam turns to Luce.*

"Go," Luce says, "I can handle things here. Harry needs it."

Miriam takes my hand, lightly, with just enough warmth to coax me back into the fringes of the living world. It takes forever to get to the edge of the nearby woods, but Miri's hand is my lifeline, keeping me anchored.

"Here, sit down. On the grass," *she says. I sit with my legs crossed, and the damp coating of dew on the ground seeps through my pants. It must be doing the same to Miri's skirt, but she doesn't mention it.*

We sit for a while, silently, her hand still loosely covering mine. My other hand is in my pocket, protected from the chill of the air around us.

"Last I heard, you were hunting down the person who did it," Miriam murmurs. "Did you…?"

"Dead. Not by me. It was the Nightwalker twins who got Johanna. I don't know who hired them, and I don't know who took them out. Odds are they're the same person."

Miriam's eyebrows knit together. "The Nightwalker twins? I thought they were unkillable?"

"I thought so too. But I found their ashes."

"Oh, Goddess. What about their dead man's

switches?"

"It was a feedback loop. Thing One says Thing Two will know who killed her, Thing Two says Thing One will know who killed him. And on and on and on."

It's like I can look up and see the recordings again, projected onto the dewy air in front of me—a ghostly man and a woman all in shifting, flowing black, same build, same buzzcut, speaking just out of sync as they stare past my head at a camera that's no longer there. The surrealism of it bringing me to my knees in a shabby apartment with all the lightbulbs blown out and a layer of singe across every surface. Breaking me.

Inspiring me.

I close my eyes and wipe the images away, but the emotions remain. "Everything feels like a dream," I say out loud.

"That tends to happen." Miriam squeezes my hand. I fight the urge to come back fully to her, to the real world. Everything seems like a dream, sure, but that's not necessarily a bad thing. As long as I float and pretend that I can wake up, I can deal with this a little easier. I think.

"Thank you for being here," I say. "For me. You really don't have to."

A huff of air, and she smiles at me. "I don't have to. But I want to. You're my friend, Harry. Plus I'm still flattered that you used to have a crush on me."

My face is stretching weirdly, and it takes me a moment to realize I'm smiling. It feels wrong. But then I see the relief on Miri's face, and a puff of air blows out of me, and the smile settles itself that much more firmly on my lips. There's tears too, escaping the corners of my eyes *to roll down my cheeks at a sluggish crawl.*

"Here," Miri says, pulling a handkerchief out of nowhere. She dabs one tear off my face and I'm suddenly overwhelmed—I don't know what I ever did to deserve someone like her. To deserve anyone taking care of my useless self, when I couldn't—when I couldn't even—

"It's not your fault, Harry," Miri says, firmly, instantly reading and interrupting the thoughts scrawled across my face. "You had no idea. It's not your fault you couldn't save her. It was never your fault."

I've already spent hours fighting with her over this point, so I keep my mouth shut. Part of me wants to argue anyway. It's the part that hates myself for every mistake I've ever made and secretly, secretly wants nothing more than to hear Miri defend me the way she defends anything she loves—passionately, with the fury of a supernova. But I can't ask that of her. It's selfish to even consider it.

Miri lets me take the handkerchief from her and press it to both my eyes, staunching the flow of tears by brute force. I can still feel the burning of salt under my skin and my eyes feel like sandpaper, but it's better than outright bawling. I offer the handkerchief back to Miri.

"Keep it," she says.

"Wait, really?"

"Of course. I brought it for you."

"Oh. That's…" Sweet. Kind. Wonderful. I don't know how to put it into words, so I lean forward and hug Miri instead.

Soft, damp fabric clutched in my fist. The scent of lavender from Miri's hair, faint in the way it's bound up tight in her bun and oppressed by the chill, but still there.

I'm all awkward, knobby limbs. She's all warmth and security and self-assured peace.

"Miri," I mumble, staring past her shoulder to the branches of a faraway pine tree. "If—if I were to fuck up, really badly…"

"It wasn't your fault."

"No, I know, this isn't about that." I pull away from her, but can't quite look her in the eye. "I'm talking about—later. The future. If—if I mess up—" I risk looking back up.

Her face is a perfect sculpture of patience. My will crumbles.

"…Never mind."

"Harry, it's okay. Whatever it is, you can say it."

"Just—never mind. Forget it." I pick at a clump of uneven grass near my hand, shrinking away from the way her eyes are boring holes into my skull.

She huffs. "Fine, if you won't talk, I will. I'm not going to tell you everything's going to be alright, because you know I don't believe in that bullcrap. And, Harry, you know I—I don't make friends easily. And I don't keep them well either. Don't lie, even you thought I was a killjoy when we first met. But even in the most uncomfortable times, you were always there for me. That's what I want to do for you too. Be there for you, unconditionally. Do you understand?"

My heart sinks. "Unconditionally?"

"Unconditionally. Call me anytime and I'll be with you, okay? Or, better yet, come over. We'll lock ourselves in my room and finally get around to cracking open that bottle of overpriced grape juice."

In my surprise, I completely forget to avoid eye contact. "You kept that?"

"Well, what else was I going to do with it? It's a thousand-dollar bottle of French wine that was corked before either of us was even born, it wouldn't be cost-efficient to drink it all by myself. I can't put it back in the cellar either—my family doesn't know we committed grand theft vino in the first place."

"Three whole years and they still haven't noticed?"

Miri is trying to stifle her giggles behind a cupped hand; it's not working.

We're so busy snorting with laughter that we nearly miss the shout wafting over from the ongoing funeral. Miri perks up.

"What was that?" *I ask.*

All previous mirth is wiped off of Miri's face. "They're burning the casket. We should go." *She rises to her feet, straightens out her skirt, and pulls me up to join her.*

"You go first," *I say*, "I'll catch up." *She looks at me a little strangely for that, but then her eyes become sympathetic. She nods and turns to leave.*

I watch her go, her dark shape molding into the small crowd that is her family. Simultaneously, four mages gather in a rectangle around the casket and draw fire into their hands.

They won't burn Johanna's body. They'll burn a *body, but not Johanna's—because Johanna's corpse is resting in the freezing basement of the house where she died, exactly where I left it. I didn't even bother to learn the identity of the random cadaver I stole from the morgue as a replacement. It doesn't matter. What's important is that, once the casket and its contents are reduced to ashes, no one will be able to tell there was a difference.*

Miriam's handkerchief is still clutched in my right hand. I stuff it into the pocket of my suit jacket; as I do, my fingers brush the smooth, curved surface of the vial I picked up from the bank this morning. The glass seems to grow hotter at my touch, as if its crimson contents recognize me.

If this is all a dream, this is how I'll wake up. This is how I'll save her. Johanna isn't gone, she hasn't left me, and I know that deeper in my heart than anything I've ever known in my life. I'm going to bring her back to me. I'm going to make things right again.

Everything is going to be alright.

CHAPTER 10
WRAPPING THINGS UP

I rub dry blood off my top lip as I watch two of the burlier Merestis carry Tristan's limp form down the mansion stairs, toward what I assume is their depressingly unkinky torture dungeon.

"What're you going to do with him?" I ask Miriam as she stands stiffly beside me.

"Make an example of him." Fire flickers in her eyes. "Your little curse-in-a-bottle is nothing compared to what we'll put him through. I'll make sure of that *personally*."

I eye Miriam's clenched fist, the silver chain peeking out from between her fingers.

"What're you going to do with that?"

"We'll keep it in the mansion, at least for the time

being. The gator moles have been through enough. It was our lapse of security that got them involved, and we don't have the right to impose anything further on them." She holds up her palm and takes a moment to be preoccupied with the shining silver. She hesitates, then looks back up. "Walk with me?"

It's an invitation, not an order. I accept wordlessly, following her as she turns down another one of the mansion's endless hallways.

"Are the Lockharts going to be any trouble?" I ask.

"Of course they are. They'll always be trouble, and we'll be trouble right back. It's how these things work."

The hallway turns a corner. I speak up. "About the gator moles—I'd like to pay them reparations of some kind. I've still got a fat envelope of rich kid money back at my apartment—"

"We know. It won't make much of a difference. What Tristan gave you barely made a dent in his ridiculously padded trust fund, and since he broke his bloodsworn oath, that money is ours to distribute. We're already using it to rebuild the gator moles' tunnels and food supply."

"Oh, okay." I duck my head, feeling a little silly for mentioning the money at all.

"...But I'm sure Shiny will appreciate the gesture."

The gentleness in Miriam's voice makes my head jerk up in surprise. She turns away in an instant, barely letting me catch the softened slant of her eyebrows and the loose set of her lips. I stare at her for just a little longer, watching the way the light of the hallway shines off her cheekbone as we keep moving. Then we enter a darker stairwell, and I turn away to watch my footing instead.

We make it down to a vault, one with an impressive, circular steel door. There's a combination lock outside, one that makes you choose between sigils rather than numbers. Miriam turns the lock carefully, muttering words I can't hear or understand, the seal on her wrist faintly glowing. Something *click*s—Miriam attempts to turn the wheel holding the enormous door closed. I hurry forward to help her; the steel gives, and the wheel begins to spin.

The door opens. The air is saturated by a low, full humming, the song of a hundred magical artifacts and heirlooms cohabitating in a single room. Miriam enters. I take a step back.

"What are you doing?" she says.

"This is your family's vault, Miriam. I'm not supposed to be here."

"Well, I'm ordering you to be here, so you don't have a choice. Get your ass inside."

I raise my eyebrows. "Yes ma'am." I hop over the threshold to join her.

Rows upon rows of glass display cases on pedestals, like the one I saw in the gator mole tunnels, line the black-coated walls. The lighting is dim enough that I can't see the edges of the room from where I'm standing. As Miriam leads me deeper in, I consider peeking at the place through my glasses just once—no, bad idea. I'll probably be blinded for life.

There's a number of empty pedestals toward the middle of the room. Miriam uncovers one and gingerly lowers the sword onto it, letting the chain coil around and around the sword in a glittering spiral. She replaces the glass case, and an application of her seal causes the whole thing to click shut.

"There," she says, "So that's done with."

We stand in front of each other for a silent, awkward moment. Neither of us can quite meet the other's eyes. I pluck up the courage to speak first, even though my voice cracks on the very first syllable.

"I'm—sorry, Miriam. This was all my fault. It doesn't matter what happened between us, I should have told you as soon as Tristan came to me. Taking the money was just an *unbelievably* shitty move. I put your whole family in danger because I couldn't handle the thought of confronting you again, and I just… I'm sorry."

Miriam is quiet for a moment, her head ducked so that I can't see her eyes.

"…I'm sorry too."

My forehead wrinkles. "For what?"

She meets my gaze, wavering a little bit, but refusing to look away any longer. "I wasn't exactly… telling the whole truth about what happened when you were in the hospital. Well, I wasn't lying. The flowers and the card, telling you not to contact me—I stick by those decisions. There was nothing else I could have done at that point. But… later. I promised that I would call when the coast was clear. And before that, I promised you, as your friend, that I'd stick by you. Unconditionally. I made both of those promises when you were in a vulnerable place, and I knew they meant a lot, but…"

"But in the end they just weren't practical. It's okay, I get it. I really do."

She shakes her head. "That's not what I meant. I definitely wasn't on the best terms with my family after your trial, but it only took about a month or two for them to forgive and forget. Well, mostly forget. After that I was free to do anything, really. I could have—should have—called you, like I said I would. At the very least, I should have let you know I was available, and that I still cared. But I—I started hearing things, scary things, about how you were doing." She finally rips her gaze away and turns her head, hugging her own arms with tense shoulders.

I stand and stare at her, not comprehending for a moment. Then the memories come flooding back—stumbling through the street with just enough strength to get to the next bar or bedroom, every mirror showing me a new cut or bruise I didn't remember earning, trying not fall asleep, don't fall asleep, don't fall back asleep…

Miri is speaking again, so quietly I almost miss it. "…and the look on Luce's face when I brought up your name… like she couldn't sleep for fear that when she woke up, you'd already be dead in a gutter. And I... I couldn't do it. It was just a phone call, but I kept putting it off. Telling myself I was busy. Avoiding it, avoiding you. I don't know how I justified it—maybe I thought you'd be angry at me for being gone so long. Or maybe I really thought you couldn't be saved, and that trying would just hurt me too. Or maybe I was scared of seeing you in a way I'd never seen you before. I—I don't know. Eventually, you seemed to be doing better, but by then so much time had passed that it was easier to just... let it lie. So I did.

"You were right, Harry. I did abandon you, and I wasn't even honest about it. I owe you an apology for that, and... I'm sorry."

...Ah, crap, I'm going to cry again. I try to blink the tears back, but fail miserably and end up forcing them out instead. "Miri," I manage to choke out, wiping my face on my sleeve. "That—that wasn't your fault, I can't believe I—shit, I'm such an idiot, I didn't even consider what the people checking up on me might think, I—I don't even know what I would have said to you if you'd called—"

She cuts me off with a raised palm. "Oh, but don't you dare think I'm letting you off the hook for all the stupid shit you've done. Demon blood, Harry? Really? What were you *thinking*?" My laughter gets lost in a wet hiccup. "Also—thirty thousand dollars? You sold my family out to that pathetic little bottom feeder for *thirty thousand dollars*? What, was the prospect of my unholy wrath not intimidating enough for you?"

My vision is still blurry from the tears, but, gods, I can't stop grinning. "Rent isn't cheap when you don't live in a giant family mansion, Miri. Besides, I only sold you out for two days."

Miri crosses her arms and tilts her head up, sniffing almost imperceptibly. In the dim lighting, I only catch a half-second glimpse of shimmering liquid in her eyes. "You are *such* an asshole." She walks forward, arms still crossed, right into my chest. I stumble back; she's not the least bit apologetic. "Goddess, I missed you."

I wrap my arms around her and hold on tight.

We spend another minute like that, both trying our hardest not to sniffle into each other's clothes, both becoming grosser and sweatier by the second. I guess dusty, centuries-old vaults aren't the best place for prolonged body contact. Eventually, the air gets stuffy enough that it's difficult to breathe; Miriam pushes away from me, half-smiling, half-grimacing, using her thumb to swipe a speck of mascara off her cheek.

"This is so embarrassing. Come on, if we're really doing this, we're going all out."

I let her lead the way across the room again, a little puzzled, but not objecting. There's a spring in her step now, something airier than her previous urgent, purposeful gait. We reach a pedestal at the very corner of the room. Miri stoops to reach into the shadowed space behind it, and her hand emerges carrying a very, very expensive bottle of wine. She turns to me, the corner of her tinted lips raised.

My stomach flutters. "Is that…?"

"Yes, it is."

"You hid it in your family's *vault*?"

"Isn't that the function of a vault? To hide valuable and stolen things?"

I shake my head in disbelief. "Can we even drink that? It's been in here so long, what if it's been infused with arcane explodey energy or something?"

Miri shrugs, the very picture of nonchalance. "We'll take our chances."

There's a ledge of sorts where the floor of one side of the room is more elevated than the other. Miri kicks off her heels and sits on it, then beckons for me to join her. I do.

"Don't we need glasses?" I ask as I shrug off my coat.

"I doubt there would be much of a difference — not one we could tell, anyway. Besides, I'm not in the mood to be sophisticated."

She clicks her fingers. With a hollow *pop*, the cork jettisons itself out of the bottle's mouth and into her hand.

"Holy shit, you *have* to teach me that trick."

"It's elementalism, silly. You wouldn't be able to do it."

She winks, then brings the bottle up to her lips and takes a swig. She swishes it around in her mouth a little, squints, and swallows. "Huh. Smooth."

She passes the bottle to me. I take a drink the

same way she did, tasting the barest hint of her cherry-flavored lip tint on the rim. I don't know what my taste buds were expecting—bitterness, a slight acidic burn? But the wine slips down my throat like the lightest, sweetest spring water, the scent of grapes wreathing the air around my head. I swallow and stare down at the bottle. "Woah. That doesn't taste like wine at *all*."

"Magic," Miri says, nodding solemnly as she takes the bottle back from me. "It's a Hell of a drug."

We keep passing the bottle back and forth, taking smaller sips. Miri's posture becomes more and more relaxed, and I can feel a bit of warmth starting to creep into my cheeks and forehead.

"So," Miri says as I pass the bottle to her, "Why did you do it?"

"Do what?"

"Try to bring Johanna back."

I open my mouth to object, but she shakes her head.

"Don't try to deny it, you know that I know. Everyone does. You absolutely attempted necromancy—with demon blood, of all things. Don't tell me you were badass enough to get ahold of that yourself." She takes a sip as she watches for my response.

"No, the demon blood was one of Johanna's old treasures. I inherited it, after she…" I pause. Close my eyes. Take a deep, filling breath. "…after she died. I somehow got it into my head that it was the solution to everything, that I could use it to make things right. And, honestly… some desperate, irrational part of me believed that this was all just another one of her tests. That if she were really, truly dead, I'd be able to feel it and accept it—and the fact that I couldn't meant that she was just hiding somewhere, watching me. Waiting for me to stop crying, put on my big girl shoes, and get to work."

Miri raises an eyebrow. "What, you figured she had a summer house set up in the astral plane or something?"

I shrug. "We're talking about a woman who had a vial of demon blood chilling in her bank vault."

"Good point." Miri sneaks in an extra sip before handing the bottle over. "I still can't believe none of us knew what you were up to until it was too late. You can keep a damn good poker face when you want to, Harry. Goddess, you're lucky Luce was there to save you. From the blood *and* from the Council."

Even Hell knows your sister was covering for you.

I rap the side of my head with my knuckles, willing Lilith's smug voice out of my brain. "Luce is a great sister. The best."

"Mm-hmm. Buy her a big fucking bouquet of roses. The purple ones that she likes."

"Yeah, okay, I'll do that." I take a swig of wine. Toss the bottle from hand to hand. "Speaking of bouquets—I still can't believe you didn't invite me to your wedding."

Miri tilts her head quizzically and squints. She doesn't seem to have heard me clearly. "My what?"

I chuckle, the wine going straight to my head. Strangely, I don't feel weird bringing this up with Miri. I actually feel more relieved. "Your wedding. You know. With Silas?"

Miri blinks owlishly at me. Then she blinks again. Then her eyes grow as wide as dinner plates.

"Oh my Goddess. Harry. *Harry*. Silas is married to my *brother*."

...I lose my grip on the wine bottle. It drops to the floor and bounces once, sloshing wine onto the carpet—I catch it before the rest spills out, but the damage is done. My entire face is on fire.

Miri bursts into peals of delirious laughter, tipping back onto the floor with her bare legs flying up into the air. She keeps cackling while I bury my head between my knees, desperately willing my body to vanish from visible existence. Puzzle pieces are falling into place without my permission: Silas's anxiety over Pax's illness, Miriam's attempt to comfort him in the study, his refusal to leave the infirmary while the bombs were going off...

"I'm such a *dumbass*," I moan into my knees.

"You thought—you actually thought—Harry, you absolute—" Miri is laughing so hard she can't even get the words out.

And then I start laughing too. I don't know if it's the wine or the stress of the day or both, but suddenly I'm giggling so hard that my entire body is quaking.

Things are a bit of a giddy blur from that point on. Miri and I catch each other up on our lives since the trial. We take turns balancing the wine bottle on top of our heads; about a cup's worth of alcohol is lost that way. I show her my scar, which she dismisses with a "Eh, it's just your neck. That's like, the least useful part of your body." But she gives it a fluttery, drunken kiss anyway, and I feel better.

I'm squinting into the bottle's depths, trying to see if there's any liquid left, when something occurs to me.

"Oh hey—you wanna know somethin' else really funny? Turns out Tristan never fucked the barriers to the sword after all."

Miri is dozing off next to me, her head gently landing on my shoulder every few seconds before she starts and reopens her eyes. "Wha'wazzat?" she mumbles, rubbing her eye with the heel of her hand. Well, she aims for her eye, but ends up smushing her hand into her nose instead.

"Yeah, i'was totally just me. Weird, right? I'm pret-ty sure iss the demon blood. Now I can punch through any magicky wall you guys put up. Like, I could probably break into one of your super-super-secret warehouses, aaanytime I want." I wave the bottle around my head in a wide, unsteady arc. "Maybe even thiss vault, if I tried hard enough. Pretty frickin' cool, huh?"

Miriam's eyes are bugging out as she stares at me, completely rigid.

"Miri? Hello? Don't do that, thassh creepy. You're seriously creeping me out right now. Miri?"

In a blur of movement, Miriam dives for the

nearest wall. A panel slides up, revealing a big, fat, red panic button.

She slams it with the palm of her hand and screams, "*SECURITY!*"

***

"Why," says Luce, "do you always feel the need to run your mouth?"

I groan into the pillow. "It's not my fault she got all weird about it!"

"Yes, of course, it's Miriam who's being weird about this." Luce's voice is dripping sarcasm all over the sheets. "It's not as though you had just revealed, with disconcerting, drunken casualness, that by your very existence you were a massive liability to her family's security. Stop squirming, you're making this more difficult than it has to be."

I'm on my stomach in my bed again, with Luce hovering over me, again. This time she has her hands pressed to the ridges of my spine and is coaxing my bone marrow to produce plasma and red blood cells to replace the pints of blood Miri and her goons took from me.

"They took samples of *everything*, Luce," I moan. "They cut off my *hair*. I have a *bald patch* now."

"Can you blame them? Honestly, it's a miracle they only took your DNA and let you go. You're lucky Miriam cares about you, because if she didn't, that family would have either slit your throat or picked you apart in a lab. Probably both, in that order."

I remember Murdoch's enthusiasm at receiving my DNA samples, her frenzied insistence that I be healed and pumped for blood again—an insistence that was stemmed only by Miriam's murderous, half-hungover glaring. I shudder.

Luce presses two fingers against the side of my throat and pauses, measuring my heart rate.

"Okay, you're just about good to go," she concludes, climbing off of me. "There's a lot of oxygen going to your head right now from all the fresh blood. It might feel weird, but don't do anything—"

I immediately scramble upright in bed. At the last second, I think to grab a pillow and hold it to my stomach, concealing the sigil that Luce—thankfully—hasn't seen yet. "Oh my gods. They're going to ward everything against me. *Everything*. I'm like, freaking legendary, Luce. I've got one of the most pompous mage families in New York scared shitless of me. Dude, I can do *anything*." The last word comes out in a scratchy, hoarse whisper. I bring my hand to my throat, puzzled at the sudden burning I find inside.

"Drink," Luce commands, raising a water bottle to my lips. I try to take it from her, but my hands are shaking. "You're body's used up a lot of water, you're dehydrated. Also, you're still slightly tipsy."

I gulp down three-quarters of the bottle, then remember something urgent. "Luce," I say, "Luce."

She sighs. "What?"

"Miri said I should get you—flowers, she said I

should get you a big fucking bouquet of flowers. Flowers, Luce."

Luce raises an eyebrow. "For what?"

"For saving my useless ass."

She snorts and smiles. "She's damn right." She gets up to go to the bathroom. "Buy me a new petticoat too while you're at it, will you? Not one of the cheap ones. Real, quality lace."

"Yeah, okay." I hear the bathroom faucet running.

Hm. There was something else I wanted to do. I drop the pillow and shrug on a half-buttoned shirt as I wobble out of the bedroom and into the living room, toward my desk. Matches, matches, where are my matches? Aha! I strike up a flame and bring back my fire sprite.

"Hi," I say, peering at it. "You. I've got a name for you. 'Tinkerbell.' How does that sound?"

The sprite—Tinkerbell—does a gleeful little shimmy.

"...I am proud of you though," Luce says as she emerges from the bathroom into the bedroom. "Harry? Where are you?"

"Uh, over here!"

"Oh, there you are." I quickly hide the matches behind my back as she comes into the living room. "Like I said, I'm proud of you. You got the bad guy, made up with Miriam, figured out something new about your magic. Though your long-suffering sister did have to jump through hoops to help you along."

"Uh, yeah."

Luce looks up and sees the awkward grimace on my face.

"Harry," she says. "What did you do?"

"Nothing, I—"

With an enormous splintering sound, two legs of my desk buckle. The whole structure lists to one side, like a made-to-scale reconstruction of the *Titanic*—and then hits the floor with a pronounced CRASH! As Luce and I stare, Tinkerbell emerges from the wreckage, clearly quite pleased with itself.

"...Tell me you plan to keep enough of Tristan's money to pay for that," Luce says.

"I. Um. Kind of promised it all to the alligator moles."

"The alligator *whats*?"

"I told you about them earlier, they're like, these albino star-nosed moles with teeth—"

Luce holds up her hands. "No, no, I don't even want to hear it. You're fine now, so I'm going home, and I'm going to sleep. *You* can deal with this mess."

And she marches out the door.

I blink after her, still holding a cluster of blackened matches in my hand. The smell of ashy smoke is starting to waft up from the floor.

Muffled laughter outside the window—I swivel and catch a glimpse of wild, dark hair disappearing from sight. My hand goes to the closed shirt buttons over my stomach. The carved sigil underneath is tender but healing, and I absentmindedly trace its path with my fingers as I stare out the window. I already have one scar I regret. Is this going to be another?

A *CRASH* from the bedroom interrupts my thoughts. Fire-extinguishing now, troubled contemplation later. The shirt that Tinkerbell ate through earlier is conveniently lying under a pile of desk-splinters—I retrieve it, wrap it around my hand as a gauntlet, and go hunting for trouble.

STEPHANIE AHN

HARRIETTA LEE: BLOODBATH

COMING SPRING 2019

STEPHANIE AHN

ABOUT THE AUTHOR

Stephanie Ahn is an author and college student who tends to write about young-ish adults just trying to get by in life. Wonder where she got that idea? She and Ink live in LA with their kid, Amara, who is also a small and feral cat.

If you would like news on the continuation of the series, please visit:
www.stephanie-ahn-books.com
where you can sign up to receive an email when the next book is released! You can also find Stephanie on Twitter @ahn_writing and on Tumblr @delphiiwrites.

Made in the USA
Las Vegas, NV
20 February 2025